Lock Down Publications and Ca$h
Presents

I0664170

THE BUTTERFLY

MAFIA 3

When It Rains It Pours

Written By
FUMIYA PAYNE

First Edition 2024

Printed in the United States of America

Lock Down Publications
P.O. Box 944
Stockbridge, GA 30281
www.lockdownpublications.com

Like our page on Facebook: Lock Down Publications
www.facebook.com/lockdownpublications.ldp

Stay Connected with Us!

Text **LOCKDOWN** to 22828 to stay up-to-date with new releases, sneak peaks, contests and more…

Like our page on Facebook:
Lock Down Publications

Join Lock Down Publications/The New Era Reading Group

Visit our website:
www.lockdownpublications.com

Follow us on Instagram:
Lock Down Publications

Email Us: We want to hear from you!

DEDICATIONS

Dear Shawn...

I was literally at my lowest, while in desperate search of my God-given purpose/I'd often question if my existence was worthless, as I could find nothing of value buried beneath my surface.

My will was gradually fading, for in the sea of my sorrow I was fully submerged/until one day I was inwardly encouraged to paddle through the pain with pronouns and verbs.

I can so clearly recall my fear and uncertainty when first starting out/how my confidence was plagued with boils of bleakness and scabs of self-doubt.

But although my nerves were as skittish as those of a newborn kitten's/with an apprehensive hand I began to pen what was already written.

And there's no way I can weigh the weight of your feedback to my debut story/your words inflated me with strength and gave me a glimpse of God's merciful glory.

I'm wholly convinced you were used to revive the weakening pulse of my withering spirit/I was suffering from an emotional disease, and your restorative remarks were able to cure it.

You vaccinated me with valor, within the web of validation you left me entangled/so not only am I eternally grateful, but I'll forever regard you as my own personal Angel.

Rest In Peace, Queen!
Yours truly,
Fumiya Payne.

Chapter 1

"My father?" Noni sourly repeated. "Nigga, if you don't get the fuck on. I ain't got no father."

He smirked. "And you must be Noni."

She tightened her grip on the gun and growled, "Don't come up in here acting like you know nothing about me. Because I promise you don't."

"My name is Anthony Randall," he looked at both her and Asha. "I'm assuming Regina never mentioned me, but me and your mother were together, before I went and did a dime in Jackson. She would send pictures every Christmas, with a short report on how y'all were turning out. And let's just say, she made it clear that Noni was the more 'outspoken' one."

Noni looked over her shoulder. "Twin, you hearing this shit?"

Asha barely nodded, her gaze never straying from those of their alleged father's. "Shawna will you give us a minute, love?"

Once they were alone, Asha cut straight to the chase. "Why are you showing up after all these years?" Contrary to what he assumed, Regina had in fact made mention of his name.

As if that was a question he anticipated, Anthony readily replied, "When your mother -"

"Say Regina," Asha sternly interrupted him.

He slightly frowned, but put aside his curiosity and correctly continued, "When your mother got pregnant, she said the only way she wouldn't get an abortion was if I never came around. She said it was bad enough you'd inherit my genes, but that she wouldn't allow my lifestyle to put y'all in danger. And since I only knew one way to eat at the time, I had no choice but to honor her terms."

Unsatisfied with his answer, Asha replied, "You said you did a dime in Jackson, and I'm guessing that means ten years. So not only did you get out while we were still young, but Regina has been dead over four years now. So, I'm sorry, but, your excuse don't hold water."

The bright one indeed, Anthony smiled to himself, recalling Regina's description of their eldest child. "You're right," he admitted to Asha. "There's no excuse I could offer to justify my absence. But the fear of rejection is hard to overcome. And I know its selfish thinking, but I thought to reach out and be rejected was far worse than to not reach out at all."

"Which brings me back to my original question," Asha said. "Why are you here?"

Anthony drew a deep breath and slowly exhaled. "Understand I'm not here to seek sympathy, but to simply be totally transparent. So with that being said... I've been diagnosed with cancer. And in not knowing what the future holds, I just want to go to my grave knowing at least I tried."

Asha literally laughed. Not at his condition, but at his audacity.

When his eyes darkened in response to what he assumed was mockery, Noni icily warned him, "Nigga, I'll treat you like the stranger you is. Don't ever look at my sister like that again."

Asha held up her hand in apology. "Nah, that's my fault. And I wasn't laughing at your sickness, but at the fact that that's what made you man-up. Because if we keeping it real, then your reason for coming here is not even from the heart. You only here to clear your conscious - just in case."

"Y'all got every right to be upset and have negative feelings towards me. But understand that sometimes it takes a strong dose of reality before we see the bigger picture. And in my case, it wasn't like I didn't want to be a part of your life. But I had been out of it for so long that I wasn't sure if you'd even accept me in it. Not to mention, I have no other children or a father of my own, so I didn't even know where to start."

"Listen," he quickly continued before Asha could respond, "I've put down some of the most vicious demonstrations in Detroit, over which I feel not one shred of remorse. But not reaching out to y'all is a mistake I truly regret. And I'm not expecting you to outright embrace me, but I'm asking that you give me however long it takes to make amends for my cowardly behavior."

Despite his spiel sounding sincere to the ears of Noni, she waited to hear how Asha would respond; for her sister had always had her best interests at heart.

Asha regarded the man for a thoughtful moment, then motioned for Noni to put away her weapon. When Noni complied, Asha held out her hand for her sister to hold. This was her baby, whom she'd fiercely protect with her very own life. And it was important she painted a clear picture for Anthony.

"I can't say I'm saddened by the news of your health," Asha truthfully began, "because for real, I don't even know you. But I don't wish that on no one, so I do hope you get better. But as far as you making amends, I'm afraid that's something you gon' have to take up with God."

Anthony hadn't really expected to win them over on the initial encounter, so he offered Asha some time to reflect. "Listen, this was all unexpected, I get that. And I know how sometimes our emotions can play a role in our decisions. So, why don't you just take some time to think it over? I'll leave you with my number, and you can reach out when you're ready to talk."

"I've already thought it over," Asha looked him square in the eyes. "I thought it over for years. Years of waiting on you to show up and save us. But you never came. So I realized it was on me to play your position and protect both me and this girl right here. You abandoned us, nigga. On purpose."

As Asha got emotional, Noni got angry. She hated to see her sister upset.

"But we made it without you," Asha proudly proclaimed. "We leaned on each other and figured it out. And yeah, it might've been tough, but in the end it taught us that all we need is each other. And it's crazy how you can come up in here and boast on your 'vicious demonstrations', but yet you didn't have the courage to come save your own flesh and blood. And you can't imagine what we went through. So for you to show up now, it's like a slap in the face. But like I said, I hope you get better, but ain't no room for forgiveness in my heart. We fought our demons alone, and I suggest you do the same."

He digested her disclosure before looking at Noni. "And what about you? You unwilling to give me a chance, too?"

Noni smirked, "You clearly don't know. Nigga, me and my twin share the same heart. So if she say ain't no room for forgiveness in hers, then it damn sure ain't no room in mine."

Anthony slowly bobbed his head in acceptance. "Well, I guess there really isn't much else to be said, then, is it?"

"I guess not," Noni coldly confirmed.

He smiled before turning to leave. "I was hoping for a different outcome, so I won't act like I'm not disappointed. But I gotta admit, for two young women who did it alone, I couldn't be prouder. So consider me a fan who'll be rooting from afar."

A former hitman with a graveyard of kills, Anthony Randall was fully aware of their ruthless reputation. In keeping an ear to the streets, he would proudly listen to the countless accounts of their felonious behavior. And until the day of his demise, he would curse himself for not coming forward sooner - as he was certain that him and his daughters could've created a dynasty.

"And one other thing," Asha called out, as he was on the verge of leaving.

When he turned to face her with a glimmer of hope, she coldly crushed it with a word of advice. "Continue to do what you've done over the years."

As his mind made sense of what she implied, Noni gave him a hand. "What she means is... stay the fuck away from us. We don't need you, nigga."

Watching him leave, both girls were eyeing the door in deep thought, when Asha turned to lay a hand on Noni's cheek. "You good, love?"

Noni nodded that she was. "And you?"

Asha shrugged, "I don't feel nothing for him. And I don't plan on giving it much thought. I buried them emotions a long time ago. But maybe it would've been different if he said he'd been locked up all this time. But to hear him say he could've been showed up... girl, fuck that nigga."

"Then, fuck that nigga," Noni cosigned.

As they left to get Shawna, Asha wore a subtle smile while staring at the floor; for she now understood her initial alarm to Anthony's unsettling aura. With his inherited genes swimming through their bloodstream, her and Noni were cut from the cloth of a coldblooded killer.

They found Shawna out at the bar, where Asha immediately took notice of D'Aura's absence. "Ain't nobody still heard nothing from D'Aura?" She asked the bartenders, to which they shook their heads.

"And this definitely ain't like her," one of the women spoke up. "So I hope everything okayay."

Asha took Shawna aside. "I need to leave you in charge, while I shoot over to D'Aura's crib really quick. Lo-Lo ain't here, so it's on you to step up."

Fearful of something going wrong, Shawna nervously stuttered, "But - but -"

"Ain't no 'buts'!" Asha cut her off. "I need you, and that's all there is to it. So, do you got me, or what?"

Shawna swallowed the nervous lump in her throat. Asha and others had been there for her, and she knew it was time she started returning the favors. Even if trying meant losing her life. "I got you," she answered as confidently as possible.

Asha gave her a hug and kiss. "Alright, love, we'll be back in a minute."

As Asha hurried for the exit, Noni lagged back to say in Shawna's ear, "There's a gun in the safe that's already de-cocked. Go put it on you, and don't hesitate to use it if anything goes wrong." When Shawna eyed her in uncertainty, Noni added, "I'd rather see you in a cell than a cemetery. Now go do what I told you."

Noni came out the club and Asha pulled up to her in the Denali XL. She sped off before Noni could get settled in her seat.

They rode in silence to D'Aura's house, where Asha threw the truck in park and quickly hopped out. Not knowing what to expect, Noni withdrew her weapon and caught up to her sister.

"I understand you concerned, but we still gotta be cautious. We don't know what we walking into."

Though Noni was right, Asha ignored the warning and banged on the front door. "D'Aura!"

When D'Aura didn't answer after a second set of knocks that would've awakened the dead, Asha removed a spare key and unlocked the door. Upon tentatively entering the darkened house, Asha turned on the living room light and went still as a statue. "Oh. My. God," she uttered in absolute shock.

Beside her, Noni stood speechless, as this was a scene she hadn't expected to encounter.

With her nakedness partially displayed through her opened robe, and her brown eyes bulged in frozen terror, D'Aura indecently hung from the second story banister.

From the pile of feces on the floor beneath her, she was definitely dead.

But that didn't stop Asha from racing up the steps with the intention of untying her.

"Twin wait!" Noni called, as she ran up the steps and physically restrained her.

"Let me go!" Asha cried.

"She dead, love. And at some point the police gon' get involved. We can't afford to leave no prints at a crime scene. I know you upset, but you still gotta use your brain, girl."

Asha sagged into her sister and bitterly wept. She didn't know when D'Aura had taken her last breath, but she blamed herself for not coming over sooner. *I might've saved her,* she guiltily thought.

"The baby!" Asha sprung to her feet with a wide-eyed expression. In their shocking discovery she'd forgotten about Polaris.

Their first stop was at D'Aura's bedroom, where Noni stood guard as Asha checked in each of the walk-in closets. As she got down in her knees to look beneath the bed, she held her breath, then exhaled in relief at the little girl's absence. But the search was far from over.

Asha checked a hallway closet before approaching the bathroom door, which was fully shut. Nervously reaching for the doorknob, she nearly jumped out her skin when Noni touched her arm.

Noni put a finger to her lips, then signaled for Asha to open the door from a sidelong angle. They didn't know what was lurking on the other side of that door, and Noni would take no chances on her sister being injured.

As Asha flattened her back to the wall and reached to turn the knob, Noni crouched, extended the weapon in both hands and braced herself for a deadly engagement.

The door swung open and gave view to what appeared to be an empty enclosure. Then, Noni stared in concern at the closed shower curtain. She considered firing a warning shot, but common sense prevailed. If there was a present threat beyond that plastic, they would've surely opened fire by now. So Noni inched further inside the bathroom, with Asha behind her.

With her ears pervaded by the pounding of her heart, Noni inhaled a deep breath, grabbed the shower curtain and snatched it back.

Gasping in horror at a heartbreaking sight, Asha covered her mouth to smother a scream.

Chapter 2

With her head tipped back and her eyes rolled upwards, Lo-Lo begged Uno for mercy as he suckled her clit like it contained flavored water. "Uno, please!" She cried, clutching the sheets in one hand and his dreads in the other.

From watching her twist and turn like a woman possessed, he was further encouraged to feast in a faster and more famished fashion. He was clearly capable of pleasing her, so why not take her to breathtaking heights?

While extending her clit with his lips, he inserted two fingers and sent them in search of her hidden G-spot. When she let out a sharp cry and spasmed in his mouth, he applied pressure to the prized location and drove her to the edge of insanity.

Amid her wildly bucking like an untamed bull, she screamed, squirted, and cursed him for being subjected to such tear-evoking torture. But in his refusal to show mercy, the more she cursed, the louder he slurped.

When she lifted her hips in an effort to force his whole face in her yoni, he replaced his fingers with his tongue and used his thumb to rapidly stroke her throbbing clitoris.

Repeatedly yelling for him never to stop, her breath quickened, her body stiffened, then she screamingly surrendered to the most amazing sensations she had ever experienced. If she was to die in that moment she'd go with a smile.

As she trembled from the aftershocks of her orgasmic explosion, he trailed delicate kisses from her navel to her neck. Stiff as a corpse, his condom-covered pole pulsed in impatience. It felt left out, and was eager to engage in the illicit festivities.

She looked down and gasped at the girth of the 8-inch limb, to which its owner proudly smiled, "He only gon' hurt you if you want him to."

She hissed as the tip pushed past the her lips of her vulva. "Baby, wait, it's too big," she whined, using her hands to obstruct him from going any deeper.

After a moment of allowing her to adjust to his size, he eased further into what felt like was furnished with a furnace. *Ain't no way this pussy this good,* he groaned to himself as she clawed at his back.

Slowly working his hips while halfway embedded in her glove-like yoni, he nibbled on her ear and encouraged her to relax.

As he continued to grind with a gentleman's gentleness, she soon gave in to her greed and shamelessly pled, "Give me more, baby. Fill me up!"

He obliged and she screamed. But as his erection examined unexplored areas, pain dissolved into pleasure and she began matching his movements in a rhythmic manner.

Peering into the windows of her soul, he was thinking on how he had never felt so emotionally connected to a woman during sex. And beneath him, she returned his stare with similar thoughts. For she, too, felt the connection, and knew it arose from having the patience to first partake in making love mentally.

"I want to get on top," she suddenly announced, to which he quickly rolled over without dislodging himself. As she sat above him with her hands on his chest for support, she grinded her pelvis in circular motions. "Do I feel good to you?" She asked with a grimace, then modified her movements to a back-and-forth grind.

Intensely focused on finishing the race, he could only nod in response. But he nearly fumbled, when she reached to remove her hairpin and shook her blonde curls free. With the lustrous mane framing majority of her face, she leaned forward and fed his mouth her dangling breasts.

Aggressively sucking her nipples in accord to her wild-like movements, he palmed her pillow-soft cheeks and inwardly prayed, *Please don't let me nut too quick. At least not on the first trip.*

As if she'd heard his desperate plea, she reclaimed her nipple and spun on his pole. Placing the soles of her feet on the bed, she gripped his shins for leverage and bounced up and down in a merciless manner.

At the provocative sight of her jiggling cheeks, he closed his eyes and fought for control. He knew that once a certain sensation came coursing through his loins, there was nothing you could do to reverse its direction.

She granted him temporary relief when she uprooted herself and crawled forward on the bed. Positioned on all fours, she looked back at him and jiggled her cheeks. "Come fuck me."

When he obediently rose and reinserted himself, she piercingly screamed as he plunged to her bottom in one heartless thrust. "Nah, don't run," he grabbed her hair and held her in place. "You finna take all this dick!"

At a long-stroking pace that sent ripples through her cheeks, he sexed her so good that she started to whimper. "Oh my god, baby, why are you fucking me like this? Please, don't stop, baby. Harder!"

After having held out for as long as possible, he felt that sensation that signaled he was seconds from spilling his seed. Releasing her hair, he gripped either side of her waist, hunched his back and hammered her insides as hard as he could.

With no way of escaping his barbaric behavior, she hollered and heaved before coming unraveled. Beginning to babble as her body convulsed, she felt heavy one minute, then the next she was weightless as she floated on a cloud of heavenly bliss.

As his lower half jerked as if jolted by volts of electricity, he came with the howl of a wounded wolf. "Gottt-damm, girl," he smacked her bottom and enjoyed its jiggle. "I don't think I ever nutted like that before. That shit was crazy!"

He collapsed beside her, as she lay face down with a case of the tremors. "What's up, Lo', you good?" He reached over to ruffle her hair.

When her heartbeat slowed, she turned to face him with a lazy smile. "I just wanna cut that thing off and keep it in my purse."

Proud of his praiseworthy performance, Uno joked, "I already know it's a drought on good dick out here. But you gotta plug now. So all you gotta do is let me know when and where, and I'ma drop this shit off on you every trip."

As Lo-Lo admitted to herself she could get addicted to the sexual high his glass pipe provided, she looked down at it. "Ugh, Uno! If you don't go take that nasty ass condom off and flush it."

He rolled towards her and grinned, "Shit, I thought you might need an energy drink. So I was just trying to be considerate and save it for you."

"Oooh, you so nasty!" She laughed, pushing him to get out the bed.

When he returned from the bathroom and climbed back in bed, she laid her head on his chest and toyed with the hairs on his toned stomach. "You be working out?"

He smiled while flicking through TV channels. "Nah, why you say that?"

"Because I was watching you walk to the bathroom, and I couldn't help but notice you gotta tight, little muscular ass booty. And your stomach -"

"Girl, you can't be looking at a nigga ass like that," he busted out laughing. "Type shit yo' lil' freaky ass on?"

Lo-Lo joined him in laughter. "Nah, babe, it wasn't like that. I was just checking you out. And I'm saying, ain't nothing wrong with a man having a nice butt. I mean, as long as it ain't bigger than his girl's."

"Yeah, well, don't be getting no ideas," his tone turned serious. "Because this mu'fucka off limits. Straight up."

"It better be," she said in assent before kissing his chest.

As she nibbled on his nipples, Uno smiled, "Aye, yo, what made you sit on that cake like that? That was some wild shit."

She looked up, "You liked that, didn't you?"

Recalling how he had licked her cheeks clean of the icing, he admitted, "Yeah, that was different."

After revealing he was the first person with whom she had shared the memorable experience, Lo-Lo straddled him and began kissing her way downwards. "Now I gotta get revenge."

"Oh yeah?" He clasped his hands behind his head. "How you gon' do that?"

"Through torture," she replied before taking him captive in the confinement of her mouth.

Chapter 3

"Girl, I still can't believe you only eighteen," Kiva told Shawna as they chilled at the bar. "I mean, you look young, but you got the demeanor of someone much older."

After noticing the urgency of the twins sudden departure, Kiva had saw the lost look on Shawna's face and correctly assumed she'd been left in charge. Presented with a visual of a much bigger picture, she cut her shift short and joined Shawna at the bar.

"Yeah, I've definitely been through a lot," Shawna admitted. "So I guess it's kind of like a gift and a curse."

"What you mean by that?" Kiva inquired, genuinely curious.

"I don't know, it's like..." Shawna thought of how to best explain it. "It's like, no little girl should go through certain things in life, you know what I'm saying. And when they do, that's what I consider the curse part of a person's circumstances. But when you're able to get through it, while learning and getting stronger in the process, then that's what I consider the gift part of it." She looked at Kiva, "Does that make sense?"

"Probably more than you know." Kiva patted Shawna's hand, deeply impressed by her outlook on life. The girl was definitely experienced for her age. Which brought Kiva to her next question. "So, how long have you known the twins?"

Before Shawna could answer, their attention was drawn to the sudden outburst from a nearby man.

"Bitch, you acting like you here for your health!" He drunkenly yelled at a woman who'd been giving him a lap dance. "Like you don't need the money. Like yo' stanking ass too good for a nigga to touch you!"

"Nigga, if you don't let go of me." The dancer attempted to pull her arm free.

"What's going on over here?" Shawna asked upon walking up.

"And who the fuck is you?" The drunk demanded, his breath reeking of alcohol.

"I'm Shawna," she bravely answered. "And I'm in charge right now. So I'm asking you to please let go of her arm. You're hurting her."

"I'm hurting her?" He repeated with a scowl, shoving the dancer away and stepping closer to Shawna. "Bitch, you don't know what a hurting is. Now get yo' black ass out my face before I show you."

Shawna considered the gun but refrained from pulling it. Instead she replied, "You think hitting a girl makes you look tough? Well, it don't. It actually make you look weak. Trying to fight somebody you know you can beat."

He drew back as if to strike her and was suddenly snatched up from behind by one of the bodybuilders Asha kept on payroll.

"Aye, put me down, muthafucka!" He barked while uselessly struggling to break loose.

In complying with the customer's orders, the security guard, Bolo, flung the fool to the floor and readied himself for an enraged reaction.

But when the drunk jumped up, not even his heart full of Hennessey was enough to drive him forward, for he sensed that the warrior before him would surely destroy him.

"Yeah, that's what I thought," Bolo grinned with a predator's gaze. "You'll flex on a female, but you ain't no match for a man. Now get yo' shit and get the fuck out of here, before I start breaking all your bones, nigga."

As badly as he wanted to spit something slick, the drunk did as he was told and gathered his things. But that didn't stop him from glancing at Shawna in wholehearted hatred.

With her expression reflecting amusement at his comical character, she simply dipped her head in a farewell gesture.

Once the drunk had departed, Bolo laid a hand on Shawna's shoulder. "Wassup, you good, lil' mama?"

Shawna nodded, to which Bolo commended her. "You definitely handled that well. You gotta think, a lot of these dudes get drunk and get even more ignorant than they already are. But you stayed calm and didn't match his energy, which in some cases only eggs them on to do something stupid."

Proud of her own actions as well, Shawna was glad she hadn't reached for the gun. By staying true to herself, she thought maybe God had decided to deescalate the drama. But Shawna's inner joy was short lived, as she received a text from Noni that was sent in all caps, COME OUTSIDE. Not knowing what to expect as she raced to the exit, Shawna dropped the gun, which had been loosely secured at the small of her back.

As if the clattering noise of the weapon overrode the music, every eye in the club seemed to turn in her direction. Momentarily froze in embarrassment, Shawna awkwardly returned their stares before snatching up the gun and fleeing out the door.

Bolo included, Kiva and several other employees were thinking along the same lines - even the quiet one keep it on her.

Outside the club, Shawna spotted the SUV and hurried toward it. From behind the wheel, Noni lowered the passenger window and signaled for Shawna to join her up front. *Where is Asha?* Shawna thought to herself as she quickened her steps.

As she hopped in the truck, ready to ask about Asha, Shawna felt a presence behind her and turned.

Wearing a spaced-out look over tear-stained cheeks, Asha cradled a blanketed Polaris while rocking back and forth. The image made Shawna recall when Asha had rocked her in a similar fashion, whispering words of encouragement as she dealt with withdrawal.

Shawna turned back to Noni with a face full of questions, to which Noni gestured for her to step out the truck.

"D'Aura dead," Noni quietly informed her, as they stood behind the Denali.

"What?" Shawna exclaimed, then quickly covered her mouth and glanced at the truck.

Noni nodded, "She hung herself. And we found Polaris in the tub. We thought she was dead at first."

When Noni had snatched back the shower curtain, Polaris had been curled in a fetal position. Along with bearing the stench of urine and feces, she had a dark, dried-up substance on her face which they had presumed to be blood. Consumed with grief over the death of a small child, Asha had reached in the tub to smooth the child's hair, when Polaris opened her eyes, took in the twins and commenced to screaming at the top of her lungs.

Both sisters were initially startled, then Asha had quickly gathered Polaris in her arms and soothingly spoke into the frightened child's ear until the screaming subsided into a less intense sob. As she held her, she was relieved by the scent of the little girl's cheeks; for the dried-up substance wasn't blood after all, but the remnants of chocolate covered candy bars. For the past three days, Polaris had survived on several Milky Ways.

"So listen, this is the plan," Noni outlined to Shawna, "You take Asha home and I'ma close up the club. I'll have an Uber drop me off."

"Noni, you know I can't drive that good!" Shawna shrieked in panic.

"Yeah, well, I guess you gon' have to put your big girl panties on tonight. Because we gotta get her home, and somebody gotta close up the club."

"But why you ain't just drop her off before coming here?"

"Because I don't want her to be alone, Shawna."

"Well, why we can't call Lo-Lo?" Shawna suggested. "You know I ain't got no license."

"We shouldn't have to call nobody that should be here. Now all you gotta do is get on the E-way. It's less traffic at this time of night, so you'll be straight."

"But them cars be doing over a hundred miles an hour, girl. I ain't ready for nothing like that."

Noni smiled, "They do not be going that fast."

"That's what it seems like."

"Well, I'm telling you they don't. But if it makes you more comfortable, just take the regular way home."

Shawna doubtfully shook her head, "Noni, I don't know."

"But Asha been teaching you how to drive, Shawna."

"Yeah, in the parking lot of Walmart."

Recalling the spiritual conversation she recently had with Ms. Johnson, Noni grabbed Shawna by her shoulders. "You know why you gon' be good?"

When Shawna shook her head, Noni answered, "Because God got you. Girl, you ain't gotta evil bone in your body. I know shit been rough for you in the past, but like somebody told me, 'God only gives the toughest battles to his toughest soldiers'. And after everything you've been through, I'll be damned if you ain't no soldier."

Shawna visibly brightened at the uplifting spiel. And Noni was right, God did have her. He always had. And just maybe her path had a purpose that required a series of hurdles to create endurance. Because after all, no medals are won without strenuous work ethic.

"I'ma get her home, Noni. Even if I gotta drive slow as hell."

Telling herself she could do it as she got behind the wheel and fastened her seatbelt, Shawna took a calming breath, put the truck in drive and gradually let her foot up off the brake pedal. "Lord, please be with me," she silently prayed while the truck coasted forward.

Though traffic was light, Shawna waited until there wasn't a car in sight before she turned out onto the street. This was much different than her parking lot lessons, which meant she had to be overly careful.

With both hands on the wheel, Shawna was several blocks from the club, when the interior was suddenly illuminated by flashing lights. "Oh my God, oh my God!" She panicked at the sight of the cruiser in her rearview.

Forgetful of her blinker as she pulled the truck over, Shawna was so scared that she couldn't even think straight. She had an unregistered gun in her purse, and she was still on probation. So she'd surely be arrested and hauled off to -"

"Just be yourself," Asha softly counseled as she continued to rock.

Before Shawna could ask her to elaborate, a male officer approached the driver side window and motioned for it to be lowered. With a pinkish complexion and steel blue eyes, his wide stance was suggestive of his readiness for action.

Shawna lowered the window and nervously smiled. "Hi, officer, did I do something wrong?"

Without returning the smile, he replied, "Can you tell me why you were doing seventeen, in a 35 miles-per-hour zone?"

Shawna couldn't help but press her forehead to the steering wheel and laugh at herself. She'd been so nervous about everything else, that she had paid no attention to the digital speedometer.

She turned back to the officer and touched her heart, "I apologize for my silliness. But to be completely honest, I'm just learning how to drive, and I can't begin to tell you how nervous I am."

"Ma'am, can I see your license and registration?"

"I don't have a license. And the truck is rented."

"I'ma need you to step out the vehicle," he ordered, taking several steps back and resting his hand over the holstered Sig Sauer.

With Shawna following his orders, the truck's interior light gave view of Asha's silhouette in the backseat. Telling Shawna to place her hands on the truck, the officer unclasped his holster before asking her who was inside the vehicle.

"Just my best friend, Asha, and her goddaughter, Polaris."

He warned Shawna not to move, then cautiously approached the truck for a closer inspection. Upon leaning in through the driver's side door, he peered toward the backseat area and was met with two pairs of the saddest eyes he could ever recall witnessing. From the rocking woman to the blanketed child, the officer could only imagine what had caused such sadness.

"Ma'am, are you okay?" He asked Asha, to which she bobbed her head in response. "And you or the child are not in any present danger?"

She shook her head and explained, "Shawna is like my little sister."

After a thoughtful moment of eyeing Asha and Polaris, he dipped his head in sympathy and wished Asha a good night.

Telling Shawna to lower her hands, he quietly inquired, "What happened?"

"The little girl's mother committed suicide, and she'd been left all alone for like three days."

He groaned, as he was a father himself and had a weakness for children. So though the child was a stranger, he wouldn't allow his profession to come before humanity.

"Young lady, I'ma let you off with a warning this time, but I strongly suggest you get your license before getting back behind the wheel. Now get your butt back in there and get that little girl home."

As Shawna reentered the truck and sighed in relief, this experience had just convinced her of two things: God's spirit was indeed an active force in her life, and not all cops were governed by a cold-hearted creed. Because in spite of his stern tone of voice, the officer's eyes had reflected blue pools of compassion.

Once they safely made it home, Asha asked Shawna to keep an eye on a sleeping Polaris while she went to get some air. Stepping out onto the back porch, Asha longed for a cigarette, even though she didn't smoke. This was unreal. And there was no amount of money she could spend, or people she could kill to bring D'Aura back.

As she was thinking these turn of events would somehow affect the course of her life, she realized there were two phone calls she'd have to make in the morning. One was to D'Aura's mother, and the other an anonymous call to authorities, informing them of a young woman's death.

In the parking garage of Uno's apartment, him and Lo-Lo were engaged in a passionate kiss as they stood alongside her Corvette. It was the morning after their explosive encounter, and the couple couldn't quite quench their thirst for each other.

Gripping two handfuls of her backside, Uno broke the kiss and attempted to lure her back to his apartment. "Won't you come back upstairs so I can taste that rainbow again?"

"Listen at your lil' horny ass," Lo-Lo laughed, tempted to take him up on his offer. "I told you I gotta check in with my girls. And I already know I'm in trouble. Messing with you, I stayed out all night."

"I understand them your peoples, but you a grown ass woman, Lo. And if your man trying to spend some time with you, then how you gon' deny him that?"

She leaned back in his arms, "Oh, so you my man now?"

"What, you think this shit for fun? You think I go around eating pussy for my health? I know you ain't got me mistaken for a no fucking clown."

"Of course not," she sassily replied. "Because clearly I wouldn't give my pussy to no clown."

"Okay then, so what's the problem? It ain't a mystery we got chemistry."

As much as she liked him, she wasn't ready to reveal the real reason behind her reluctance. It went deeper than the fear of heartbreak. It actually dated back to when her and the twins had been in juvenile prison.

"Uno, don't take this the wrong way, but there's some parts of my past I'm not ready to discuss. It's so complicated. And you gotta understand, I've been knowing the twins over half my life. I done been through some shit with those girls, and they've always had my back. So you just gotta give me time to figure it out. Because trust me, the feeling is mutual in regard to our chemistry."

He studied her closely before cupping her chin. "Lo-Lo, don't play with me. You can warn me now if we just passing time. I ain't never -"

"Uno, stop," she silenced his insecurities with a peck on the lips. "Ain't nobody playing with you. And just because I'm not ready to commit, don't mean we not exclusive. So from this day forward, don't be sharing that dick with nobody else. Then I'll be forced to cut him off for real."

In spite of himself, he couldn't stop smiling. "Yeah, a'ight. And you bet not be giving none of that candy away either."

"Or what?" She teasingly challenged.

Sliding his hand down her pants, he put his finger in her yoni and went straight to her spot. When she gasped in reaction, he breathed in her ear, "Don't forget about that drought. You can be plugged in one day, and cut off the next. And you know how many dicks it'll take before you find another good one?"

He withdrew his finger and sucked it clean. "*Now get*, before I bend you over in this garage."

Lo-Lo reached down to grab his crotch. "You ain't got the balls."

Uno eyed her for a sign of being silly, then scanned the garage before spinning her around. Forcing her face on the hood of the 'Vette, he snatched down her pants and easily slid inside her soaking wet yoni.

While muffling her moans with the palm of his hand, he quickly brought her to climax with rabbit-like strokes, short and fast. For him all it took was to watch the jiggling of her cheeks. As he buried his head in her hair and came with a convulsive growl, Lo-Lo removed his hand from her mouth and protested, "Uno, I know you ain't just come in me."

He kissed her neck and grinned. "Girl, I don't think it's a nigga on earth who could control himself inside some shit feel that good. So you gotta blame yourself for that one."

She pushed him off and readjusted her clothes. "Uno, I'm serious. I can't afford to get pregnant."

"I'm saying, just pop a Plan-B. But if you ask me, I think we'd make a pretty ass baby. A lil' mixed nigga, with blue eyes and a big dick."

"Boy, why you always gotta be so silly!" Lo-Lo laughingly swatted him. "And for all you know, it could be a girl. Then what, what do you want her to have?"

At his failure to respond, Lo-Lo pushed him. "Yeah, that's what I thought."

Uno smiled, "Man, that shit hit different with a boy and a girl. I ain't even gon' lie."

"I already know. But why is that? How come a boy can crack a whole crowd of women, but a girl sleep with just a handful and be labeled a hoe? That shit double standard as hell."

"It is, but I kind of understand it, though. Because it's like, the man is more masculine and grittier, you feel me. And the woman is like, softer and more sacred. Like, she got the ability to reproduce. So it's like she held at a higher standard than a man. I mean, that's just what I think."

"But if the woman so sacred," Lo-Lo countered, "Then why y'all men be disrespecting us so much? Calling us bitches and hoes like that's what's on our birth certificate. That shit ain't cool."

"You right, and I can't even debate that. But Uno sticking to the code, you hear me?"

"And what code is that?"

He grabbed her by the waist and pulled her against him. "The code of a real one. And real niggas don't hit women or belittle them with words. That's that clown shit. So it's some shit you ain't gotta worry about with me, and mistreating you is one of 'em. As God is my witness, I'm standing on business, Lo'."

Lo-Lo wrapped her arms around his neck. "I really like you, Uno. I do. But if you ever switch up on me, for even one second, as God is *my* witness, I'ma cut your ass off like a bad habit."

He dipped his head in acceptance. "Understood."

After they shared a parting kiss and agreed to talk later, Uno stepped back as she slid in the coupe. Bringing its engine to life, she wiggled her fingers in farewell before driving off.

As Uno thoughtfully watched the car exit the garage, he was startled by the sound of someone clapping in applause. He quickly turned toward the source of the sound and was surprised by the sight of his evil-minded cousin.

"That was nice," the older cousin, D-Nutty, commented, as he continued to clap while closing the distance. "And, nigga, that white bitch got a fat ass."

Masking his annoyance with a smirk, Uno replied, "What, you was on your creep shit, jacking that dick to a nigga performance?"

Offended, D-Nutty hotly remarked, "Watch your mouth, Blood. I don't give a fuck about the white bitch for real. I only came through to make sure you was safe. The homies threw you a party for your B-day, and you ain't even show up." He scoffed in disgust. "Now I know why."

Uno averted his gaze in guilt, for he had genuinely forgot. His plan was to spend a few hours with Lo-Lo, then close out the night with his comrades. But the rainbow had gotten the best of him.

"So wassup, you gon' invite a nigga upstairs, or what?" D-Nutty continued.

During the quiet elevator ride to his apartment, Uno dreaded the foreseeable conversation D-Nutty wanted to have. He knew once something was set in the man's stubborn, sinister mind, nothing short of death would deter his pursuit.

D-Nutty cut his eyes at Uno, as if he had access to the man's inner thoughts.

Once inside the apartment, where D-Nutty made himself comfortable on the leather sofa, he plucked a partially-smoked blunt from the ashtray and sparked it. After coughing up a lung from the High Octane's potency, he revisited Uno's failure to attend his own party. "When you ain't show up or answer your phone last night, the homies was feeling some kind of way. They went through a lot to get everything set up. But after I thought about it, I was able to see the bigger picture, so I convinced 'em you were taking care of some serious business. And you can thank me for that later."

"What's the bigger picture, Nutt? Uno asked, though he already knew the answer.

But he was caught off guard, when D-Nutty emphatically answered, " A takeover."

"A takeover?" Uno frowned, realizing there was more on his mind than what he assumed.

With a devious grin, D-Nutty bobbed his head at the brilliance of his plan. "I'm saying, you fucking one of the main bitches of the Butterfly Mafia. And it ain't nothing she won't tell you if you ask the right questions. We can take everything."

"And you think they just gon' let us take their shit? Like they got to where they at by being passive?"

D-Nutty scoffed, "When have you ever known a dead muthafucka to defend anything? So maybe what I should've said was... a 'hostile takeover'."

In an attempt to discourage his diabolical plot, Uno asked, "And how you supposed to keep what they got going, when you ain't even got no plug?"

"I been doing my homework," D-Nutty said as he stubbed out the blunt. "And remember that night when old girl, Noni, was arguing with that Mexican bitch at the club? Well, come to find out, that was Southwest Perez little sister. So I guarantee that's where they getting that shit from. And if they suddenly out the picture, then clearly somebody gotta pick up that slack. So, why not us, my baby?

At a loss for words, Uno doubtfully shook his head and dryly replied, "I don't know, bruh."

D-Nutty scooted to the edge of the couch. "Would you ever go against the gang, homie?"

"What type of question is that?"

"A simple one that I expect you to answer."

The two men held each other's stare before Uno stated, "I live by loyalty, so you ain't never gotta question my character."

"Well, act like it, then. Because I know you ain't gon' side with a hoe you just met over men you been marching with since you learned how to walk. I bleed this street shit, lil' nigga, and I'll die for it on *any* given day. I'ma live how I wanna live, and I don't give a fuck. If I win... great. If I don't... fuck it. But what I'm telling you is this, you gotta chance to change our life, so there should be hesitation in your heart at all. We family, nigga. And don't ever forget that. And if we put this move down right, nigga, you'll have enough money to buy you *five* white bitches!"

But won't none of 'em be Lo-Lo, Uno dishearteningly thought to himself. Stuck at a crossroad between love and loyalty, he was beginning to see he only had two options: betray a brotherhood to which he had pledged his allegiance, or double cross the woman he was falling in love with. But whichever direction he decided to take, Uno knew that his life would never be the same.

Chapter 4

With Asha driving and Noni beside her, Shawn sat in the backseat, holding Polaris on her lap. They were in route to Flint, Michigan, where the child's grandmother awaited their arrival.

In case of an emergency or God forbidden tragedy, D'Aura had given Asha her mother's phone number shortly after moving to Detroit. She explained that although her and the woman shared a strained relationship, she was still her mother and deserved to be notified if something ever happened. While the woman didn't sound too distraught when Asha informed of D'Aura's death, she did inquire about the safety of her granddaughter. Asha had assured her that the child was fine, to which the woman demanded her immediately delivery.

As they drove in silence, Noni glanced at her sister out the corner of her eye. Since their discovery of D'Aura, she felt the change in Asha's energy towards her. And without having to be told, Noni knew it resulted from Asha holding her responsible for D'Aura's death. Because if she hadn't been so strongly opposed to her sister's gut feeling, then maybe they could've arrived in time to save D'Aura's life. With her conscious imprisoned by the burden of guilt, Noni didn't know where to begin in expressing her remorse.

Upon their entering the slums of the small city, Shawna squeezed Polaris tighter at the sight of several houses that looked fit for demolition. She had evolved from humble beginnings herself, but this was certainly no environment for a 5-year-old girl.

Slowing the truck to a coast as she scanned the house numbers, Asha parked in front a shabby two-story that seemed incapable of withstanding a strong winter wind. When she peered over her shoulder, Shawna returned her gaze with a pleading look; as if implying there was no way they could desert this baby in conditions like these. But despite Asha's displeasure at delivering Polaris to such a depressing locality, this was her biological grandmother, who by law was entitled to custody of the child.

Exiting the truck with a heavy heart, Asha went around to Shawna's door and opened it. "This her grandmother, love," she reasoned in a tone of regret. "And she called for her."

Shawna relinquished the child in reluctance, feeling they were making a crucial mistake. Because what were the chances of fruit being produced from unfertilized grounds? People becoming products of their environment was statistically proven.

"We can come see her all the time, Shawna," Asha consoled, as she cradled Polaris on her hip. "And we'll make sure she never goes without."

With her head down as she fiddled with her hands, Shawna just nodded in response. She felt an instant attachment to the child that she couldn't verbally explain. It was her scent, her sadness, and a series of other things that instilled the desire to safeguard her from further suffering. And had the decision been hers, Shawna would've kept Polaris all to herself and given her the ultimate love all children deserved.

While carrying Polaris up to the house, Asha made her a promise that she would always come visit and bring her McDonald's. But not even the mention of her favorite restaurant was enough to evoke a response from the unspeaking child. Since being removed from the tub two nights before, Polaris hadn't uttered a single word.

As Asha ascended the porch, she heard a car door close and turned to see Noni coming towards her. "I don't need help dropping off no child, Noni," she firmly stated. But when Noni made no move to retreat, Asha sighed in annoyance before turning to knock on the screen-less screen door.

From behind her tinted window, Shawna watched as the front door of the house was opened by a figure she couldn't clearly see. Out of concern and curiosity, she hopped out of the truck and hurried toward the house. If they were to leave Polaris in this desolate place, Shawna would at least lay eyes on her designated guardian.

The grandmother, Ms. Eady, had a wiry frame with a short bush of hair that was mainly gray. Robbed of a gracious ageing by alcohol and drugs, it was hard to believe that D'Aura and Polaris were a part of her offspring.

With a cheap strand of rolled-up tobacco pinched between her fingertips, Ms. Eady cracked a lopsided grin at the sight of her granddaughter. "Y'all bring my grandbaby on in here!" She pushed open the ragged screen door.

Inside the unkempt shack that harbored an unpleasant odor, the girls struggled to hide their horror at its trifling appearance. This woman was clearly allergic to cleanliness. When Ms. Eady called herself considerate and cut on a light, Noni cringed as two cockroaches scattered for safety in separate directions.

Unaware of the insects, Shawna's attention was drawn to the half-dressed man who sat on a recliner in a corner of the room. With a beer in one hand and the other indecently wedged inside his briefs, he was intensely focused on the TV screen, where a pair of bikini-clad women provocatively danced. As he sensed someone staring and locked eyes with Shawna, she quickly averted her gaze; with her heartbeat pounding in foreboding alarm.

As Ms. Eady stubbed out the cigarette and extended her arms in request to hold Polaris, Shawna covered her mouth and bolted out the house. She'd seen enough.

After handing over the child, Asha nudged her head for Noni to go check on Shawna. When she reached the truck, she found Shawna in the backseat, leaning over and crying.

"It's gon' be okayay, love," Noni rubbed Shawna's back in a soothing manner.

Shawna angrily lifted her head. "How can you say that?" She pointed at the house. "Did you see that place? Did you see that creepy ass man, sitting there in his boxers? Wouldn't no decent human beings leave a baby in a place like that. So don't tell me it's gon' be alright, because I don't believe you, Noni!"

This was Noni's first time ever witnessing Shawna get upset and she didn't know how to respond. So she told her she'd be right back, returned to the house and whispered something into Asha's ear.

Telling Ms. Eady to give her a minute, Asha followed Noni outside, where they were shocked to see Shawna walking down the street. "Shawna!" Asha called out as she ran to catch up to her. She had to literally grab her to stop her from walking. "Where you going, girl? We all the way in Flint."

With a steady stream of tears sliding down her cheeks, Shawna tried to pull free. "Let me go, Asha. I gotta get out of here. I gotta get as far away from here as possible."

"I understand you upset, but –"

"Did y'all see what I saw?" She pointed in the direction of Ms. Eady's house. "Did you see how filthy it was? That woman won't take care of herself, so how can you expect her to take care of a child? And that man... girl, I can't spot a pervert from a mile away. And you wanna know how? Because I was the victim of so many of 'em. They hurt me, Asha. They made me wanna ball up and die. And it started around the same time I was that little girl's age. And if we leave her in there, who gon' save her? Who gon' protect that baby? She would've stood a better chance if we dropped her off at an orphanage."

As Shawna fully broke down and sagged into Asha. A nearby Noni wiped a tear from her own eye. She could personally relate to being sexually violated and wished such a damaging experience on no other girl.

After Asha steered Shawna back to the truck and helped her inside, Noni quietly suggested, "Let's go get that baby, twin."

Asha frowned. "And how we supposed to do that, Noni?"

Noni partially lifted her jacket to expose the handle of her Hellcat.

"Girl, are you crazy? We can't just go in there and kill them people and take that baby. What good we gon' do her if we all death row?"

"I know you blame me for D'Aura, and I can't say I don't blame you for being mad at me. I fucked up once and I ain't gon' fuck up again. So I'm willing to sacrifice myself to save that baby."

As Asha contemplated a more diplomatic move, she recalled a recent incident and had a sudden idea. "Wait for me in the truck," she told Noni before walking back inside the house. Asking Ms. Eady if they could have a word in private, Asha winced when the woman passed Polaris to the pervert.

"Listen, ain't no way to sugarcoat this," Asha began as they stood on the porch, "so if I offend you, I apologize. But the thing is, my girl, Shawna, done got attached to that baby. And not to be judgmental, but I don't think it would be in the child's best interests if she was brought up in this type of environment either. Not to mention the trauma she's dealing with from losing her mother."

"Which is all the more reason she should be with her Granny," Ms. Eady replied, placing her hands on her narrow hips in defiance. "And just because I don't live in some big ol' house doesn't mean I'm unfit to raise no child. My own granddaughter, at that. So don't think you come up in here on your high horse and look down your nose at me. Because little girl, you couldn't walk a block in my boots."

Ms. Eady looked Asha up and down before grabbing the screen door. "Thinking you could just take my grandbaby away from me. What the hell wrong with you?"

"It could've been beneficial for everyone, ma'am. That's all I was saying."

"Beneficial? What could I possibly benefit from giving you my grandchild?"

Asha shrugged, "That would've been up to you."

Ms. Eady narrowed her eyes. "What you implying, girl?"

"That I would've made it worth your while."

The woman released the screen door. "Is that so?"

Asha nodded. "It is."

Her internal wheels turning, Ms. Eady considered her current circumstances. Aside from smoking rolled-up tobacco, which was nearly gone, she was forced to share bottles of beer with a man who drank like a fish. She hadn't been high in over twenty-four hours, and the first of the month was still a whole week away. So she could either take on an extra mouth she couldn't afford to feed, or take advantage of the opportunity standing on her front porch.

"You look too bougie to be dabbling in drugs," Ms. Eady incorrectly assumed, "So how much money we talking? Hypothetically speaking."

"Whatever you feel is fair," Asha replied, ready to bring the bargain to a close.

From her visual assessment of Asha's attire and the shiny vehicle in which she travelled; Ms. Eady decided she would shoot for the moon. "I want five thousand dollars."

"Five grand?" Asha feigned outrage at the amount.

"And that's nonnegotiable," Ms. Eady added. "Because let's not forget we talking about my grandchild. My only grandchild."

"And how I know you won't report her missing after I give you all that money?"

"Because I expect you to bring her to see me from time to time."

After eyeing the woman for a trace of dishonesty, Asha concluded it was a risk worth taking. And though she didn't think the woman would set off an Amber Alert, she could see her seeking more funds in the future.

"Go get her," Asha said before walking off the porch.

Asha's bargaining idea came courtesy of their trip to Columbus, Ohio, where Shawna had offered money to a frustrated mother for custody of her kid. While that woman had been appalled by such a proposal, Asha had hoped that Ms. Eady's indigence would elicit a different reaction, which it had.

When Asha climbed in the driver seat, Noni lifted her head in a questioning manner.

"It's under control," Asha simply replied, as she removed a loaf of bread from the center console. In midst of her peeling off blue-colored bills, Noni leaned over to quietly inquire, "She sold her to you?"

Bobbing her head in answer, Asha closed her hand over the money and hopped out of the truck.

Planted on the porch, Ms. Eady had a firm grip on her granddaughter's hand as Asha walked up. And she had no intention of releasing it until the payment was in her palm.

Watching Asha's hand like a hawk while she counted out the money, Ms. Eady was angry she hadn't requested more.

"Five grand," Asha announced upon completion of her count and held it out.

"Girl, would you lower your voice. I don't need the whole neighborhood all up in my business." After sneaking a peek over her shoulder to ensure the coast was clear, she snatched the money and released her granddaughter's hand. "And I'm serious," she told Asha while stuffing majority of the bills in her bra and the rest in her pocket. "I expect to see this child sometimes. Now gon' and get out of here, before my conscious kick in and I change my mind."

"That woman something else," Asha smirked to herself, as Ms. Eady hadn't even thought to kiss her granddaughter goodbye.

Standing outside the truck, Noni opened the backdoor as Asha approached it with Polaris in hand. "Hey, Shawna," Asha leaned inside the truck, "Somebody wanna see you."

When a tearful Shawna slowly rose up from the third-row seating, Asha picked up Polaris and sat her inside the truck.

"Polaris!" Shawna rushed to embrace her chubby little body. "Oh my God, baby, are you okayay?"

Barely able to breathe from being so tightly squeezed, she nodded her head against Shawna's chest.

As she cradled the child with a motherly tenderness, Shawna looked up to Asha with the most thankful expression; for she would cherish Polaris to the degree she had desired during her own childhood.

Chapter 5

Beneath a starry dark sky in Detroit, Asha turned down the street on which their house was located. After a circling of the block, she was on the verge of pulling into their driveway, when she stepped on the brakes.

Eyeing her sister in concern, Noni's hand automatically moved toward her waist. "Wassup, twin?"

Asha thought for a second and abruptly pulled off. "Something ain't right."

By now, Noni had the Hellcat in plain view. With her forefinger fondling its trigger, she watched her side mirror for the appearance of headlights.

Once they had merged into traffic on a main street, Noni asked Asha what had aroused her suspicion.

"I don't know," Asha shrugged. "I just know something wouldn't let me turn in that driveway."

Unbeknownst to them all, a dark colored car had been parked by their house. Slouched in the front seat were Hotrod and Dogbite, who both had handguns that held thirty rounds. They had been camped out since nightfall, planning to ambush the twins upon them coming home. When they saw the truck pause before suddenly pulling off, they assumed they'd forgotten something and would soon return. But they were certain of one thing, this was indeed where the twin sisters lived.

Before hanging D'Aura with the belt of her robe, Hotrod had used her daughter as leverage to gain information on the twins. He assured D'Aura that her child would be spared if she simply revealed the location of the twin's residence. Not knowing Hotrod had already sanctioned her daughter's death, D'Aura did what most mothers would do in hopes of saving their baby.

Lo-Lo was standing outside her house as the Denali drove up. Behind the anxiety she heard in Asha's voice over the phone, Lo-Lo packed a pocket rocket inside her jacket. She had never discharged it but would readily do so for the protection of her people.

When the three girls exited the truck, with Noni holding a firearm and Shawna carrying a child, Lo-Lo grew increasingly curious at the puzzling sight. Something was definitely going on.

Inside the house, where they placed a sleeping Polaris on the couch before gathering around the dining room table, Lo-Lo took in the downcast expressions on each of their faces. When it was clear neither one of them intended to talk, Lo-Lo impatiently questioned, "So is someone gon' tell me what's going on? I mean, clearly I'm curious."

There was a moment of silence before Asha softly spoke up. "D'Aura killed herself and left the baby in the bathtub."

At Lo-Lo's shocked reaction, Asha went on to reveal the list of events that transpired over the past forty-eight hours. When she explained the part about purchasing Polaris for a monetary payment, Noni directed a look of displeasure in Lo-Lo's direction; for these were things she would've known had she not been distracted.

As Lo-Lo contemplated the disturbing disclosures, Noni rolled her eyes and sighed in irritation. "Girl, if you don't stop looking like that?"

"Looking like what?" Lo-Lo asked.

"Like you concerned and shit. Just stop with the faking, please."

"Faking?" Lo-Lo indignantly repeated. "I ain't gotta fake bone in my body, and you know that."

"Would y'all lower y'all damn voices," Asha sharply cut in. "This the longest that baby done slept since we got her. And I don't need y'all waking her up."

"But like I was saying," Noni continued in a quieter tone, "If you wasn't chasing that Uno nigga around, you would've been here to help out. Got Shawna doing everything, damn near about to have a nervous breakdown."

"Noni, I was not about to have no nervous breakdown. I just got a little emotional."

Lo-Lo looked to Asha for support. "Girl, you know I would've been there if had known y'all needed me. I admit I lost track of time, but you should know I would never purposely not be there for y'all."

Though Asha refrained from mentioning the number of times she'd initially called Lo-Lo's phone, she was definitely disappointed in her untimely absence. She was allowing a man she just met - with unknown motives - to interfere with an oath to which she pledged her loyalty.

"Leave my mama alone! Leave my mama alone!"

Startled by the child's sudden outcry, the four girls turned to see Polaris on the couch, jerking her head from side to side as she underwent a nightmare.

Shawna ran over to the couch and gently shook her. "Polaris, baby, wake up."

When her eyes blinked open, she looked at Shawna and began fighting for her life. "Let me go! Let me go!"

Not knowing what else to do, Shawna grabbed her and held her close to her body. "It's okayay, baby, it's okayay. You're just having a bad dream," Shawna repeatedly consoled her until Polaris stopped struggling and fell back to sleep.

While the girls stood around the couch, watching Polaris as she now peacefully slept, Shawna quietly stated, "I remember what made me have nightmares, but I wonder what's causing hers?"

As her mind drew conclusions based off instinct, Asha was almost certain that the earlier activation of her inward alarm was somehow connected to the little girl's nightmare.

With going to sleep completely out of question, the girls quietly sat in the living room, watching a muted episode of Love & Hip Hop. Shawna was planted right next to Polaris, who she silently vowed to protect by any means. Lo-Lo had her feet tucked beneath her, wondering how to handle the clash between her allegiance to loyalty and her longing for love. Noni was sat on a recliner near the front window, with the Hellcat in hand and a heart full of guilt. And Asha - who had her arms behind her back as she earnestly thought - slowly paced the floor in deliberate steps.

It was two hours later when Polaris reopened her eyes. "Hey, sugar bear," Shawna softly greeted while rubbing her hair. "You hungry, baby?"

Polaris shook her head, to which Shawna replied it was important that she put something on her stomach. "You've hardly eaten anything in days, and it's not healthy, baby. So will you be a good girl and at least try to eat a little bit? Please."

As the unresponsive child just stared at her lap, Asha stopped pacing; for something had dawned on her in regard to the little girl's behavior. Approaching the couch, she stooped before the child and asked, "Polaris, do you remember when you told me you loved me on the phone?"

Several seconds passed before she slowly bobbed her head in recollection.

"Look at me, Polaris," Asha tenderly urged. Upon her doing so, the reflection of sadness in her eyes hurt Asha to her core. But she fought through her emotions and forged ahead. "When I told you I loved you, too, I really meant it. And I'm so sorry for what happened to your mama, but I know she would want for us to take real good care of you. And the only way we can do that is with your help. I need you, Polaris, so will you help me, baby?"

Recalling her mother once telling her to be a good girl for Asha, Polaris agreed to comply by way of a subtle nod.

Asha took one of the child's hands in her own. "Baby, did you see anybody hurt your mama in any kind of way."

Holding their breath in suspense, the girls groaned in sympathy when Polaris bowed her head and slowly nodded.

"I know you don't want to think about it," Asha continued, "But I need you to tell me what happened."

There was a lapse of silence before she softly spoke. "The bad man hurt my mama."

"And how did he hurt her?"

"He hit her and made her fall."

"And then what?"

"I tried to make her wake up. But the other bad man grabbed me and picked me up. He made me get in the tub. And he said if I got out, they would hurt my mama again."

"Is he the one that gave you the candy bars?"

Polaris nodded.

Thankful for the thug having compassion for an innocent child, Asha wrapped her arms around Polaris and squeezed her. "You're such a brave little girl." She kissed her forehead. "And your mama would be so proud of you."

While keeping the child close to her bosom, Asha glanced at her girls as it now made sense. Not only hadn't D'Aura purposely abandoned her baby, but the culprits who killed her were likely the same ones who'd set off her intuitive alarm.

Shawna and Noni exchanged a look, as both girls were genuinely grateful for Asha's instincts. Because had she turned into that driveway, where an ambush likely awaited them, they knew there was no turning back once you've been turned into a memory.

Along with being grateful, Asha was concerned. She knew for a fact that Dullah was buried beneath six feet of dirt, so who was the fierce-hearted foes who was focused on first degree murder? A question to which she couldn't currently answer, she would control what she could and move forward accordingly.

Handing Polaris back to Shawna, Asha gave Lo-Lo the option of packing a few personal belongings. "Because this right here ain't safe."

"But D'Au -" Lo-Lo caught herself in mid-sentence, as she was mindful of Polaris being able to hear.

Already knowing the direction that Lo-Lo was going, Asha took her aside and further explained, "It don't matter if she knew where you lived or not. Let's just assume her death is related to us, and that she was convinced to tell everything she know. And with thinking like that, what sense would it make not to take our wellbeing seriously? No matter how smooth we think we might think we be moving, we not untouchable, Lo'."

"But where we gon' go?"

"The safest place I could think of," Asha answered.

Chapter 6

"A hotel?" Lo-Lo exclaimed as they turned into the MGM Grand in downtown Detroit. "Asha, how can you hardly consider this the safest place?"

"I mean, just think about it," she replied while parking near the front entrance. "This the top hotel in the city, which means they got top security. And from what I read on Google, they gotta private lobby. So if you're not a guest, they all over you. But more importantly, in a hotel this big, there's no telling what room we could be in."

In the backseat, Shawna smiled in pride at Asha's thinking. The hotel idea was ingenious, as it basically ensured they could sleep peacefully at night. Because what were the chances of bandits booting in a door at the MGM?

There was a female employee behind the front desk of the hotel's lobby. Appearing to be in her mid to late twenties, she was an attractive woman whose name tag read, Symphony.

"Hi." Asha flashed her a smile as she approached the counter. "I'd like to rent a room."

Symphony returned the smile and asked if she was looking for something in particular.

Asha named the Grandview Executive Corner Suite, which overlooked the downtown area from the hotel's top floor. Measuring 1,000 square feet, the suite included a living room, dining room, separate baths, and a host of other amenities associated with luxury living. Despite its nightly four-figure rate that would dip into the Mafia's monthly profits, Asha perceived precaution as priceless. Because what good was money if you wasn't alive to spend it?

After informing Asha of the suite's availability, Symphony asked her how long she intended to stay, to which Asha answered, "I'll start with a month."

Symphony looked up as if she hadn't heard her correctly. "Girl, did you just say a month? A full thirty days? No disrespect, but you do know how much that thing cost, don't you?"

Asha smiled as she removed her debit card and state ID from her pocket. "You know I Googled y'all." She passed the plastic to Symphony. "Now gone and charge that thing for a month."

As Symphony looked from the card to Asha and back at the card, Asha could see she was skeptical, but took no offense. "I wouldn't jeopardize your job, love. But I understand I'ma stranger and you couldn't possibly know that. So to calm your nerves, just call your manager and let them come take care of it. Because trust me," Asha grinned in good nature, "My shit just as legit as PNC bank."

Promising Asha it wasn't personal, Symphony picked up the phone to summon her manager. Then, she paused to peer up at Asha, "Do I really gotta get these white folks involved, girl?"

Asha warmly smiled at a woman who undoubtedly had a decent heart. "I won't be offended if you do. But to answer your question, as a real woman, I wouldn't even put you in a situation like that."

After a thoughtful moment Symphony replaced the receiver. "I'm telling you now," she warned Asha while filing the debit card into the computer, "If this shit come back to bite me on my ass, I'ma make sure I come bite you on yours."

Asha laughed at the image of bitten on her butt. "Ooh, not on the ass, girl!"

Accepting the key card to the suite, Asha voiced her gratitude before knocking on the countertop twice in farewell.

As Symphony watched her exit the hotel, she couldn't but wonder who the younger woman was. How was someone her age able to afford their most expensive suite for an entire month? She was entertaining various possibilities, when Asha reentered the hotel, trailed by three females and a small child.

When the well-dressed group boarded the elevator, Symphony slipped her phone from her purse. While it was against company rules to engage in personal affairs during your shift, she was too intrigued for self-restraint. Logging on to social media, she typed in the name *Asha Kincaid.*

Despite the circumstances of their stay, the girls were duly impressed as they entered the suite. With a panoramic view of the city, the room was worthy of lodging royalty.

As Noni made a beeline for the bar in search of a bottle, Lo-Lo took a quick tour and returned to complain, "It's only one bed in here. How we all supposed to sleep in one bed?"

Asha shrugged as if that was the least of her worries. "I don't know, I'll get some good air mattresses. But if it's that important, you can sleep in the bed with Shawna and the baby. I'm just trying to make sure we safe, girl."

Quiet as usual, Shawna went to go place a sleeping Polaris in the king-size bed. Since revealing the source of her nightmares, the little girl was already showing emotional improvement. In fact, she had taken several bites of a breakfast burrito on their way to the hotel. Asha had made the right call when encouraging her to talk, as it allowed the release of a bottled up terror that had been torturing her 5-year-old mind.

To Noni's dismay, the wet bar was absent of alcohol. Determined to get her a drink, she found the number for room service and literally ordered a case of Bel Aire. If they were going to be holed-up in a hotel, for who knew how long, she would make sure she was stocked with her favorite champagne.

Between her sister's excessive drinking and Lo-Lo's appetite for a man's affection, Asha didn't know which behavior bothered her most. But being she could tackle only one issue at a time, she'd begin with the problem that posed the severest threat.

Nudging her head for Lo-Lo to join her, Asha led the way to one of the bathrooms. "Close the door," she instructed, taking a seat on the edge of a large tub.

Lo-Lo complied and turned to inquire, "What's going on?"

"Do you believe in your heart I love you, unconditionally?" Asha asked in all seriousness.

"Of course," Lo-Lo unthinkingly answered. "Why would you even ask that?"

"Because I need you to trust me, Lo'. I need you to trust that I got your best interests at heart, even if you don't agree with me."

Lo-Lo looked away, for she dreaded the direction the conversation was headed. She had known it was coming and wanted to avoid it for as long as possible. Or at least until she had come up with a solution.

"We're like lambs amongst lions," Asha continued in a reasoning tone. "And I'm speaking from a street-level perspective. Girl, what ear out here ain't heard of Butterfly Mafia by now? And how many people you don't think plotting on how they can take our spot? No matter what we do, these men gon' always see us as just a group of girls, which to them is equivalent to an easy meal."

"Yeah, I hear you, but -"

"This ain't nothing you can debate, Loretta," Asha cut her off. "Girl, you think you falling in love, but you falling weak. Don't you know these niggas think they can take what we got by force or finesse? It's like we tight roping over a lion's den. And it's only one way to get across, by trusting no man."

In spite of the spiel making perfect sense, Lo-Lo wasn't ready to relinquish her hold on what she thought was true love. "I hear everything you saying, Asha. Believe me, I do. But I'm telling you, Uno ain't like that. I promise he got a good heart."

"But what about the hearts of his people? Can you vouch for theirs, too?"

Lo-Lo was thinking of a rational response, to which Asha stated, "You could keep thinking till you turned blue in the face. Ain't no getting around it. And even if he told his people you was off limits, do you honestly think they would listen? Because of our position, we're targets now, Lo'. And if you keep hanging around this man, you gone be a target that's easily accessible."

"But I got feelings for him, Asha. So what am I supposed to do, just turn 'em off?"

You were never supposed to turn 'em on! Asha inwardly thought, but instead she wisely replied, "Most times our hardest decisions, be our smartest decisions. So for the sake of your sisters, I'm hoping you'll do the right thing."

Before leaving Lo-Lo to deliberate over her decision, Asha left her with an additional word of advice, "At the end of the day, you a grown woman. Which means you're entitled to do whatever you please. But in being mindful of the Mob, please don't bring danger to our doorstep."

Lo-Lo sighed in frustration as Asha closed the door behind her. She had a difficult decision to make. She could take sides with loyalty and forsake a man who had tunneled his way into the core of her heart. Or she could choose love and forsake a sisterly oath she had vowed to uphold. She was damned if she did, and damned if she didn't.

***

It was 11 PM and Symphony's shift had officially ended. As she was telling her replacement she'd see him on Monday, the ding of the elevator drew her attention. She quickly excused herself when its door slid open, and Asha stepped off.

"Girl, why you ain't tell me?" Symphony grinned as she ran up to Asha.

Asha looked at her, confused. "Tell you what?"

Symphony had enough sense to lower her voice. "That you, Butterfly Mafia."

Despite being totally caught off guard, Asha maintained an unreadable expression. She thought about playing dumb, but decided it was pointless. This clearly wasn't a case of the girl just making a good guess. She knew something.

Symphony addressed the sudden awkwardness with a confession. "Listen, I'm sorry for being nosy, but it's not everyday someone your age come in here and rent our biggest room. So I got curious and looked you up on social media."

"But I'm not even on social media."

"Your sister is. And after fighting that dude on camera, she lightweight on some famous shit out here for real."

While scrolling through Noni's IG account, which she made sure to follow, Symphony couldn't believe she had checked the Butterfly Mafia into her hotel. Aside from the twins being rumored as ruthless, Symphony heard them be described as a female movement that strived to empower.

Asha accompanied the girl outside, where she joined her in her grayish sedan. It was a two-year-old hybrid manufactured by Hyundai. "Can I talk to you, Symphony?" Asha turned in her seat. "You know, like, off the record, and between just us?"

"Of course," she readily answered. "I might be a little nosy, but I'm far from a GQ."

"A GQ?"

"A Gossip Queen, girl."

Asha lightly chuckled at the befitting label. "I like that. And especially because a lot of people don't understand the sacredness in silence. There's the saying, 'the fish can't get caught if it don't open its mouth."

Symphony groaned at the wisdom of the proverb. "Mmm, that's deep."

"And it's real," Asha included. "Girl, you know how many people talk themselves right into a frying pan? Just watch First 48. And all because they can't control that little ass tongue in their mouth. But you gotta remember, the human mind is divided into three categories: small, average, and great. So there's certain shit you gotta expect from certain people."

"What do you mean, three parts?" Symphony inquired with an earnest expression.

"So you got small minds, average minds, and great minds," Asha explained. "The small minds discuss people. You know, that GQ shit. The average minds, discuss events. Like, sports, religion, politics, shit like that. But the great minds, the great minds share ideas. Like, how to improve character, gain generational wealth, and whatever else that involves progress in life."

Recalling the DOB on Asha's state ID, Symphony was awed by the depth of her intellect. The girl had the mindset of a matriarch. No wonder she could afford a month-long stay at the MGM.

"So what was it you wanted to talk to me about?" Symphony eventually asked, as she was submerged in suspense.

For the sake of her safety, Asha chose to just slightly bend the truth. "That little girl you saw is my goddaughter. And not even a week ago, she watched her mother get murdered by a jealous boyfriend."

As Symphony covered her mouth in horror, Asha continued, "He basically found out that the little girl wasn't his and flipped out. But luckily she was able to run and hide before he could hurt her, too. She's been having nightmares ever since. She thinks the bad man coming back for her. So until they can catch him, or I can figure out what to do next, I decided this was the safest place for us right now. I gotta protect that baby, Symphony, and he gotta go through me before he get to her."

Symphony lent Asha a supportive hand. "I gotta little girl myself, and I can't even imagine her going through something like that. I know there's nothing I can say to lighten the severity of your situation, but just let me know if there's anything I can do to help."

"Thank you, girl, I really appreciate that. And for real, all I need you to do is keep our whereabouts on the hush. Because there ain't no doubt in my mind that that man is capable of hurting a child."

"You got my word," Symphony solemnly swore. "And if I see or hear anything that don't sound right, I'ma be the first to let you know."

Expressing her appreciation as they embraced, Asha withdrew a wad from her windbreaker. "This a token of my gratitude."

Symphony shook her head in refusal. "You ain't gotta pay me for doing what's right. Because if roles were reversed, I hope you'd do the same for me."

She official. Asha smiled to herself, as the offering of money was a mere test of character. Had Symphony accepted it, Asha would've been forced to seek shelter somewhere else. Because how could trust the word of a person whose principles came with a price?

After they exchanged another embrace, Asha wished her a safe weekend and exited the car. She waved goodbye as Symphony drove off, then walked over to the Denali and climbed inside. Taking a moment to relish the silence and solitude, she then played the pain-laced music of her favorite male rap artist, Rod Wave.

As he rapped about the challenges of balancing the ups and downs of life, Asha let her seat black, closed her eyes and reflected on the past few days. First, there was the unforseen encounter with her father, who she refused to forgive for neglecting his familial duties. Despite part of her wanting to give him a shot at attaining redemption, she could neither excuse nor ignore his intentional absence.

Next was the thought of D'Aura, whose death she was certain was entirely her fault. Aside from it likely being linked to her lifestyle, she cursed herself for allowing Noni to interfere with her instincts. *I probably could've saved her*, she said to herself for the thousandth time.

With her thoughts now revolved around the difficulty in raising a child, Asha was startled by an unexpected knock on the passenger window. It was Shawna, who wore an apologetic look for her interruption. And she hadn't meant to sneak up on Asha but was simply concerned about her emotional health. Though Asha was the type who would smile through the pain, Shawna sensed she was mentally strained from the weight of the world that rested on her shoulders.

Asha popped the locks and Shawna hopped in. "I didn't mean to scare you, love, but I was worried about you. But if you wanna be alone, I'll leave."

Smiling in fondness at a big part of her heart, Asha reached over to stroke Shawna's hair. "You're a real Angel, you know that? And I gotta strong feeling in the end you gon' be the one that keep us afloat."

As Shawna inwardly doubted she could fill Asha's shoes. She remembered Puma once saying she had more inner strength then she gave herself credit. With her two favorite friends having faith in her character, maybe self-doubt was a crippling disease it was time for her to cure.

They sat in silence for several minutes before Shawna spoke. "Asha, I gotta question."

"And hopefully I gotta answer."

Focused on the fidgety hands on her lap, Shawna said, "Lately I've been like, you know, thinking about when we first came up with the Butterfly Mafia. Remember we said it was about endurance and evolvement? We would endure the struggle, and eventually evolve into beautiful butterflies."

Although she vividly recalled the exact conversation, Asha was lost. "I remember, love, but I don't understand what you're asking."

Shawna's hands went still as she turned to face Asha. "We got more money than we imagined, and a club so pretty that people can't get enough of it. But yet we still take risks that could rob us of everything... our lives included. We say The Mob is a movement, but it's like, in what direction are we really moving in? Because at the end of the day we can only end up in one of two places, heaven or hell. So I guess what I'm trying to ask is, what are we doing, Asha? Like, what is the real true purpose of the Butterfly Mafia?"

Chapter 7

When they treat you like you the strongest it make you the weakest, preach/ The one that's always gon' come thru when anybody need it, I got you/ Damn, my pride so big that if I need it I keep it a secret, I'm good/ So if I ever ask for help that I mean I really need it, facts...

It was the following morning and Asha was solo as she slid through traffic, vibing to GloRilla's, "Out Loud Thinking". She hadn't had a wink of sleep, as her mind was held hostage by Shawna's unsettling question; a question to which she had provided no answer.

Minutes later, Asha turned into a small, nondescript diner, where she parked beside a white, Church van and killed the engine. As she stepped out the truck, Reverend Daniels unfolded himself from the adjacent vehicle.

After they exchanged a firm handshake and brief pleasantries, Reverend Daniels led her into the restaurant and chose a corner booth that offered a view of the entrance. He exercised faith in the Lord, but also in the firearm fixed beneath his long-sleeved robe.

"So, what's on your mind, little sister?" The Reverend implored. When she had called him at the crack of dawn and asked if they could link up, he readily gave her the diner's location.

Before Asha could answer, an older waitress approached their table with menus and a smile. "Good morning, Reverend, will you be having your usual?"

"Not today, Marianne. If you could just grab me a coffee and two sugars."

"And you, pretty lady?" The waitress turned to Asha, who said she'd be fine with a small glass of orange juice.

In between sipping her juice, which tasted freshly squeezed, Asha asked the Reverend if prayer was as effective as people made it seem.

"I'd say it depends on the motive, along with the condition of the individual's heart. I don't believe we should ask God for help in doing dirt, nor do I believe he'll give ear to the prayer of a person who is pure evil. But, keep in mind, these are just my opinions. Because I've never met no one who has personally spoke to him. But why do you ask?"

In response to her reluctance to answer, he leaned forward and urged, "Gone and spill it."

Asha looked up. "Spill what?"

There was a hint of humor in his coal-colored eyes as he replied, "The tea, young lady."

Asha giggled. "Rev', what you know about spilling some tea?"

"My congregation ain't exactly filled with old heads. Now start spilling, the suspense killing me."

Asha regarded the Reverend with a look of endearment. Because in spite of his barbaric background, his behavior toward her always bordered on respect and affection, which led her to wonder if he had children of his own.

"Rev', I feel lost," Asha quietly confessed. "It's like, at one point, I had it all mapped out. But now that I'm where I thought I wanted to be, I'm realizing it comes with too many risks. And for me, personally, I favor family over fortune. But it's like, how do you backtrack once you're so far in?"

He asked her if she was familiar with the saying 'Mo money Mo problems', to which she nodded. He splayed his hands. "It's just that simple. And for someone in the streets, the problems are significantly increased. Because there's the circling vultures who prey on weakness, the people whose job it is to bury you in jail, and a long list of others who smile in your face but can't wait for your downfall. You see, the -"

He kindly waved off the waitress as she was approaching the table and continued, "The game has changed, little sister. It's no longer designed to be dominated, at least not by people who put principle above personal gain. Just think, the streets will embrace a known snitch with the same amount of love and respect as it will a person of pure integrity. So where's the logic in thinking the streets offer longevity?"

Asha could only nod at the validity of his spiel. With so many negative currents that came with the game, it was senseless to think you could outswim all the others who had drowned in its unmerciful waves.

"There's no doubt in my mind that you're strong willed and very intelligent," the Reverend expressed. "But the fact that you're sitting here right now just means that beneath your bravery is a heart of compassion. And that speaks volumes about who you are as a person, because you could've easily adopted the 'out for self' mentality of your surrounding environment. So I'm led to believe that this meeting was already arranged."

At Asha's puzzled reaction, he went on to explain how God has soldiers in all shapes, shades, and sizes. "But people and religions are so judgmental that their ignorant to the fact that God will recruit you in his army whether you're from the slums or the suburbs. Because the thing is, He doesn't expect us to be perfect, but to simply be the perfect version of who we are as individuals. Meaning, if you're a leader - lead with loyalty. And if you're a follower - follow with faithfulness."

Although he spoke from a spiritual perspective, Asha perceived the message as one that even an atheist could apply, just be true to who you are.

"Everything you're saying makes perfect sense, Rev', but one of my girls just got killed and I don't know who did it, or even if it was because of me. So now it's like, I lead by loyalty, but how do I lead my people to safer grounds? Like, how do I stop from losing someone else?"

"That's a discussion you need to have with your Creator. Remember I once told you, when the student is ready the teacher will appear. Well, if you wasn't ready, this meeting would've never been scheduled."

"But I've never prayed in my whole life," Asha admitted. "And I don't wanna seem like I'm running to Him now just because I got problems. That's why I was hoping you could pray for me. I can tell you got strong faith or whatever, so I know He'll listen to you."

"Just because He'll listen doesn't mean He'll act. He wants to hear from you, personally, Asha. It don't matter that you coming with problems. What you think He here for? To help us in times of need. That's why He referred to as our Heavenly Father. But often times when we need help, we tend to look everywhere... but up. Not knowing it says in the Bible that He knows the number of hairs on our head. I promise you, little sister, with someone like Him on your side, you can't lose."

He saw she was seriously thinking it over and further remarked, "Understand something, Asha. He's calling for you. So at some point, the conversation gone happen. And I think you'd prefer it be through prayer... rather than in person."

Asha met his gaze upon hearing the latter part of his statement; for the occurrence of her murder was actually something she had recently considered.

Chapter 8

Flint, Michigan

Draped in black, the Butterfly Mafia wore wide-brimmed hats and large shades as they marched up the steps of a Baptist church. Despite the potential dangers of their public appearance, Asha had been firm in her decision to say farewell to a fallen friend.

Grasping the door handle with a gloved hand, Asha paused to straighten her posture, drew a deep breath and entered the church.

Heavy in attendance, the attendant's attention were drawn to the all-girl group that stepped single file down the center isle way. Upon the pastor pressing pause on his delivery of the eulogy, you could hear the squirrel-like chatter of curious onlookers.

With a rhythmic 'clack' of her Red Bottom heels, Asha led the way past the pews and up to the customized casket in which D'Aura lay. Unbeknown to the crowd, Asha was responsible for the white-and-gold purchase, along with the extravagant flower arrangement. While she couldn't reverse an event that would surely haunt her for life, she could send D'Aura off in true celebrity fashion.

Pleased at what the funeral director had done with D'Aura's features, Asha reached in the casket and brushed a caressing thumb over the coldness of her cheek. "I'm so sorry, love," she tearfully whispered. "And I can't bring you back, but I can make sure your daughter gets the best life as possible."

After regarding D'Aura a moment longer, Asha bent to kiss her forehead and inwardly vowed, *And if I find out who did it, I'ma fry 'em like catfish!*

Asha stepped back, allowing her girls to step forward and pay their respects. Though D'Aura hadn't officially been declared a member of the Mob, her contribution to their cause earned her a praiseworthy character.

Dipping her head at the pastor for the ill-mannered intrusion, Asha spun on her heels and headed toward the exit. Behind the dark lenses of her glasses, her eyes combed the crowd in curiosity; as she wondered if the perpetrators were present.

Midway down the aisle, Shawna happened to glance to her right and went breathless at the sight of a pair of green eyes that were trained in their direction. Grateful for the shades, she recognized the face of a female named Mecca. With her heartbeat pounding in fear and surprise, Shawna forced herself not to look back.

Having predicted the twins would make an appearance, Mecca peered across the aisle and unleashed her dogs with a subtle head-nod.

As Hotrod and Dogbite exited the pew in pursuit, Unique disapprovingly cut her eyes at Mecca, for she thought they had agreed on the suspension of violence. *We got the whole world in our palms. So why is this girl so determined on giving it back?*

Armed with a modified handgun, Hotrod had quickly concocted a simple plan. He'd ambush the twins in traffic. They'd eventually have to stop for a light, where he'd pull alongside them and empty his clip. With his cartridge containing just under fifty rounds, even Stevie couldn't miss such a close-range attempt.

Upon Hotrod and Dogbite hurrying out the church, it was somewhat comical how they slammed on their brakes and stood stiffer than statues. Appearing before them was a startling sight neither man had expected to encounter.

Bearing military weapons and murderous expressions, Double-O and his demons were on guard as the four girls climbed into the center SUV of a 3-car caravan. With his cargo pants tucked into tightly laced boots, Double-O took a step forward in a challenging manner. His unblinking eyes were locked on to Hotrod's, as if he somehow sensed this was the shooter from the night him and CJ had hidden in the basement of that church.

Once it was clear his invitation would go unanswered, Double-O slowly reversed to the rear SUV. *I'ma catch you, nigga,* he nodded at Hotrod before hopping inside.

Followed by her sister, Mecca came out the church as the SUVs sped off through the parking lot. "What happened? Why y'all just standing here?" She asked, displeased by the sight of the fleeing vehicles.

"What happened?" Hotrod turned to Mecca with a sideways expression. "Them bitches had the Secret Service with 'em; that's what happened. And we ain't on no suicide mission type shit."

"What? You niggas ain't got guns, too?" Mecca said in sarcasm. "Y'all shit don't work, or something?"

Hotrod smirked, as he had to literally refrain from calling her a name. "Mecca, them niggas was toting shit you see on TV. Them bullets would've went through me, came up in that church and got your ass, too. And I know that ain't what you want. So just chill and let me handle it. Because trust me, they luck gon' run out."

As she stood behind the conspiring culprits, a subtle smile played along the lips of Unique. She was once again impressed by how the twins moved. While she loved her sister to death, she couldn't help thinking Mecca might've met her match.

***

Inside a bedroom bare of the basic furnishings, D'Aura's mother, Ms. Eady, was asleep on a bed that had seen better days. As if she'd been playing possum, her eyes suddenly blinked open and she rose up like Lazarus. Something wasn't right, she was thinking to herself, scanning the room for a possible clue.

"Oh shit!" She sprung up off the mattress, recalling what it was. After a frantic search through clothing on the floor, she threw on a floral-printed dress she'd purchased from the thrift store.

With the dress on backwards as she raced downstairs, Ms. Eady found her boyfriend, Bobby, on the sofa, buck-naked. Judging from the size of his eyes, which were bigger than golf balls, the man was higher than a kite.

"Come on, Bobby, get up and get dressed. We gotta go!"

He looked from the screen of a blank TV. "Go where?"

"My daughter's funeral. Now come on, get your ass up and get dressed."

"Woman, if you don't sit your dizzy ass down somewhere. You 'bout to fuck up my high."

When he returned his attention to the blank screen, Ms. Eady grabbed his arm. "Bobby, I'm serious. Get your ass up before we be late!"

Jerking his arm free, Bobby bolted up from the couch and shoved her to the floor. "Bitch, I done told you about putting your muthafucking hands on me. Now, keep on fucking around and I'ma beat your lil' bony ass. Coming down here, fucking with people, disturbing they peace and shit."

Bobby plopped back down on the couch and reached for a crack pipe on the cluttered coffee table. "Yo dumb ass talking about a funeral," he mumbled to himself while stuffing the pipe. "Bitch, that funeral was four, five hours ago. Done came down here and blew my high for no reason."

"Four hours ago?" Ms. Eady repeated, climbing to her feet.

"It's already 5 o'clock, and that shit was at noon. She buried in the ground by now, got-damit."

Scratching her wig as she sat beside Bobby, Ms. Eady couldn't believe she had slept through her daughter's funeral. She'd had every intention on going, which was why she bought the dress. But with her primary purchase being a bag full of rocks, she had smoked herself into a crack-induced coma.

As Ms. Eady watched Bobby blow out a billow of smoke, she knew there was only one way to get rid of a guilty conscious. "Let me see that," she wiggled her fingers in request for the pipe.

With the crack-filled device fixed between her lips, Ms. Eady offered a silent apology to her daughter, then sparked the lighter and loaded her lungs with foul-smelling fumes.

Chapter 9

"And you sure it was her?" Double-O asked Shawna, who sat across from him with Polaris on her lap. Along with CJ and the other three girls, the group were gathered around the conference table in the backroom of Skittles. Currently closed, the club had become the location of BFM headquarters.

Shawna bobbed her head. "I'm sure. I looked right at her. I'm just glad I was wearing glasses, or she would've saw how shocked I was."

Aside from wondering why Mecca would attend D'Aura's funeral, Double-O was furious at the missed opportunity. Because had he known she was inside that church, he would've murdered the two men out front, and whoever else that stood in the way of him reaching the woman who had disfigured his world.

"Maybe it wasn't meant," Asha suggested, instinctively able to see his inner thoughts. "You would've ran up in that building, and they would've had your face on every news channel in the state. I know you want revenge for what she did to your friends, but how will you enjoy it if you're locked up for life? No offense, Double-O, but men not supposed to move off emotion."

Regardless of Asha being younger in age or of the opposite sex, Double-O wouldn't let his pride prevent him from listening to the wisdom of her reasoning. "Yeah, you right," he humbly conceded with a nod of his head. "Because

I definitely know men who moved wrong and ain't never coming home."

During his four-year bid, Double-O met more than a few men who had fumbled their freedom over a failure to control their emotions. And whether it pertained to women, wealth, or that thing called pride, he had heard the regret in majority of their stories. No matter how mighty a man may appear, to throw away your life over a senseless decision was a pill too bitter for a person to swallow.

As they shared speculation over Mecca's reason for attending the funeral, Asha asked Double-O if he knew where the woman was originally from, to which he answered, "I don't. I just know her sister came out the blue and got to messing with King. And it's crazy, because I remember I was at the mall with King and Unique, and we bumped into Mecca and Kavoni. And by the way they acted toward each other, you would've never thought they knew each other, let alone were sisters."

"But if they are involved, what's the motive?" Asha thought out loud, frustrated at the fact that she couldn't figure it out. "Because didn't you say what they did to Kavoni was out of revenge for their little sister?"

Double-O nodded, to which Asha shrugged in confusion, "Then, why target an innocent woman who was just taking care of her child? Like, what's the connection?"

"I can't answer that," Double-O admitted. "But I can tell that if it is her, she ain't gon' show no mercy. She orders hits on whoever... at whatever age."

Double-O went on to explain how two of the murders for which Kavoni was convicted consisted of a mother and her 9-year-old son. In Mecca's revengeful plan, she had approved the double execution just to have the murder weapon planted in Kavoni's possession.

Having heard enough, Noni loudly sighed in irritation. "Bro, why is you making it seem like she untouchable? Like she bleed different than us?" She withdrew her weapon from her waistband and laid it on the table. "You wanna know the only difference between me and Mecca... She order hits, but I carry 'em out."

"Noni, would you put that up!" Asha reproved her in a harsh tone, glancing to see if Polaris was paying attention. After her horrific experience, the last thing she needed to see was a gun. "I ain't got time for your nonsense, girl."

"I'm just saying..." Noni returned the gun to its place, feeling embarrassed.

"Kavoni the most dangerous nigga I know," Double-O declared, staring directly at Noni. "And fuck Detroit, that nigga got bodies in *multiple* states."

Unimpressed, Noni shrugged, "Okay, and you say that to say what?"

"Look where he at now. Look where being gangsta got him. And he'll tell you out his own mouth, Mecca rocked him to sleep and he never even felt it. So I say that to say, sometimes savagery alone ain't enough."

Shawna and Asha exchanged a look, both thinking this conversation was unsuitable for a child's ears. So before Noni or anyone else could respond, Asha raised her hand and called for a continuance. "We got the wrong ears in here, and we've already said way too much. So let's just hold off for a minute and we'll revisit this later. But in the meantime, stay alert and keep movements to a minimum. Until we figure this out, we gotta act like they can strike at any moment, from any angle."

Carrying Polaris on her hip as they left the room, Shawna was engaged in a quiet conversation with Double-O. After disclosing who she was, which had blown his mind, a genuine friendship had naturally come about. Their communication came with ease, as they would often share stories about Puma and Kavoni. And though Double-O couldn't resurrect Puma or rid himself of the guilt of her untimely demise, he swore not to make the same negligent mistake in regards to Shawna. He'd lay down his life if it meant saving hers.

Ray-Ray and Kiva sat at the bar as the group came from the back room. Since D'Aura's death, the two women volunteered to do more around the club. They were dancers with ambition, who saw the future rewards of being loyal to a leader like Asha.

Offering both women an appreciative smile, Asha thanked them again for watching Polaris while she attended the funeral. As much as she had wanted the child to have the chance to say goodbye to her mother, Asha had wisely decided her exposure wasn't worth it. And luckily she hadn't brought Polaris along, as Hotrod assumed that Dogbite had drowned her.

"Girl, it was nothing," Kiva assured, as her and Ray-Ray rose to give Asha a hug. "Like we already told you, just let us know what you need and consider it done. You are a strong young lady, and we backing you up one-thousand percent."

The club wasn't scheduled to open for several more hours, so Asha told Ray-Ray and Kiva they were free to take off until later that night.

Lo-Lo caught Kiva's eye and shot her a subtle headshake, to which Kiva caught on and told Asha she'd rather just post up at the club. "I'll make sure everything is ready by the time you get back. But if it's not a problem, I would like to have a few drinks, and I'll put 'em on my tab."

Asha waved off the silliness of her proposal. "Girl, you ain't gotta pay for no drinks. Get whatever you want, just do it in moderation."

Lo-Lo stepped forward and touched Asha's forearm. "I'ma stay here and help them, love. And I'll see you when you get back."

Since moving into the suite at the MGM, Lo-Lo had basically been deprived of all privacy. She understood Asha's concerns, but the prison-like conditions were taking their toll. And even worse was the lack of communication between her and Uno. Besides brief conversations during her bathroom breaks, or seldom texts messages she sent under the covers, she could count on one hand how many times she'd heard his voice.

Though she was well aware of what Lo-Lo was up to, Asha kept her thoughts to herself. Because at the end of the day the girl was grown. So she left her behind with a kiss on the cheek and a comment to be careful.

Outside in the parking lot, the girls shook hands with Double-O and CJ before going their separate ways. In spite of viewing both men as decorated soldiers, Asha saw the safety in secrecy and kept the MGM a secret. It wasn't personal, just a simple precaution.

"I want y'all to keep an eye on my girl," Asha told Double-O before getting in the SUV. "If she leave, follow her. She ain't seeing clearly right now, but it's still my job to keep her safe as I can."

He bobbed his head in understanding, pledging to provide Lo-Lo with the President's protection. "But what you want me to do if she go inside somebody crib, or something?"

She thought for a second and answered, "Call me. But hopefully she stay put and just talk on the phone, being that the club about to open up soon. But like I said, if she leaves, stay with her and hit my line 'sap.'"

Asha climbed behind the wheel of the truck, gave the men a four-finger salute and slid out the lot. As she steered through traffic - en route to the hotel, which was just minutes away, her thoughts were interrupted by an inquiry from Shawna. "We not gon' give up on Lo-Lo, are we y'all?

For fear of further angering her sister, Noni refrained from revealing her feelings on the matter. But that didn't mean she couldn't peek in Asha's direction; curious to hear what she had on her mind.

As Asha brought the truck to a stop at a traffic light on 3rd, she spoke her peace while staring straight ahead, "I love

Lo-Lo like she blood related. But at the same time, all we can do is hope she come to her senses before it's too late. Because unlike last time..." Asha paused at the memory of a past incident, "We not might not be able to save her."

Chapter 10

Flashback

After the home invasion that left their mother dead and Noni permanently scarred, the twins dropped out of high school and enrolled in the streets. Because they no longer had the basic provisions a parent provided, they were left with no choice but to get it out of the mud. Armed with collective anger and a pearl-handled pistol, their main source of income came from car jacking.

It was a warm Wednesday night, and the twins were out scouting. With Asha behind the wheel of a recently stolen Kia, the darkly clothed sisters slid through the inner city in search of a vehicle that held a higher value. Whether it was foreign or custom, they knew of several chop shops that would pay them top dollar. And there was only one rule to their felonious affair, their victims had to be of the opposite sex.

Upon them noticing a male-driven Benz that turned into White Castle, Asha made an illegal U-turn and pulled in behind it. Casually driving past as he exited the car, she saw what appeared to be a tenant of the trenches, and he was travelling alone. Perfect.

When Asha threw the car in reverse and backed into a parking space across from the Benz, Noni rolled down her toboggan which was actually a ski mask.

"Just his keys and phone," Asha reminded her sister, as she chambered a round into the semiautomatic. The purpose of taking the phone was in case the person had an app that could track their vehicle.

As the dread-headed man emerged from the restaurant with a bag of takeout, Noni threw on her hood, hopped out the car and headed towards him. The plan stayed simple; she'd state her demands, then speed off in their car with Asha trailing her to the nearest chop shop.

The man was reaching for his car door handle, when he took notice of Noni as she quickly closed in. A certified stepper from the city's east side, he stayed calm and turned to face her head-on.

"Run your keys and phone, nigga!" Noni barked, as she made the mistake of nearly touching her weapon to the tip of his nose. She was standing too close.

He calmly responded by dropping the bag and raising both hands. "You got it."

"Nigga, I said –"

With lightening speed, he slipped to his left and latched on to the gun. "Bitch, gimme me this muthafucka," he growled, as the gun discharged several times in the air.

Noni got scared as they fought for control, for she could feel her hand losing its grip on the gun. With her heartbeat pounding as she frantically thought of what to do next, there was the sound of a loud crack before the man suddenly collapsed into her, then crumpled at her feet.

Staring at his unconscious form in shock, Noni looked up to see Asha holding a baseball bat. Noni wanted to literally give her a hug, as she had never been more grateful to see her sister.

As Noni bent down to search for the man's car keys, Asha happened to look back and locked eyes with a restaurant employee who was talking on the phone. Certain the person was alerting authorities, Asha grabbed Noni's arm. "Come on, let's go!"

Speeding out of the parking lot, Asha checked the rearview mirror for signs of a cop car before approving the removal of their ski masks. Mindful of the speed limit, she forced her foot to ease up off the gas.

Noni sighed in relief once they were safely out of the area. "Twin, that shit was crazy! I can't believe that nigga grabbed the gun like that. Girl, I ain't know what the fuck to do. And like two more seconds, the nigga would've had the mu'fucka. I'll never get that close again."

"I'm just glad we had that baseball bat," Asha replied, as it was her idea to bring it along for added protection. "Because I don't know what I could've did if we didn't."

The car grew quiet at the thought of how close they had come to a potential disaster. Neither sister could imagine their life without the presence of the other. So it was either make certain adjustments to their current hustle, or look for a different, less dangerous line of work.

Ditching the Kia on a deserted side street, the twins walked around the corner to their legally owned Ford Taurus and drove home. After the White Castle encounter, they would count their blessings and call it a night.

Although it brought back bitter memories, they still resided in the Brewster projects. Being underage offered few other options right now. But the lady over management, who'd been friendly with their mother, did allow them to change units.

Raised under a roof where snitching was despised, they had refused to assist the authorities in helping them solve their mother's murder. They left out Noni's assault and claimed to have no knowledge of their mother being involved in anything illegal. "The murderer's motive were a mystery," Asha had alleged. While on the surface she appeared to be genuinely grief stricken, she was internally on fire with desire for revenge - but for only what had happened to her Noni.

As Asha led the way inside the brightly lit apartment, and Noni wielded her weapon along her left leg, the sisters stood still for a minute and just listened. In addition to cutting on every light whenever they left the house, this was another cautionary habit the home invasion created. Frustrated at being fearful every time they returned home, they agreed that when they turned eighteen and moved out the projects, they'd get an alarm before even buying furniture.

They were headed upstairs, when their heartbeats froze from a knock at the front door. Her first thought being that it was cops, Asha put a finger to her lips for Noni to be quiet. After a second knock, Asha crept down the steps and peeked through the peephole.

When Asha unlocked and opened the door upon seeing who it was, a hooded Lo-Lo and her little brother, Lance, hurried into the apartment.

"What's going on?" Asha asked in concern, to which Lo-Lo removed her hood. "Oh my God!" Asha exclaimed at the sight of her battered face. "What the hell happened?"

Speaking through swollen lips, Lo-Lo explained how an argument with her boyfriend had led to a beating. "We was at the mall and he accused me of looking at another man. And it's like, the more I denied it, the angrier he got. Then when we got back to his house, he grabbed me by my hair and –"

Lo-Lo broke down in tears and Asha embraced her. "It's okay, love," she comforted, rubbing Lo-Lo's back in a soothing manner. "You're still alive and that's all that matters."

Noni was heated after hearing the abusive account. "Lo-Lo, that's why we told you not to be fucking with that clown ass nigga!"

Asha shook her head at her sister, which Noni ignored, "Nah, twin, she need to hear this shit. Because if she would've listened, this would of never happened. Look at her face!"

The boyfriend in question, Kenny-Boy, was a known drug dealer who was six years their senior. Shortly after him and Lo-Lo first met, the twins asked around about Kenny-Boy's nature. Needless to say, the streets were unanimous in declaring him a clown. He was said to be the type who measured manhood by materialism and money, rather than character and creed.

"Look at me, Lo-Lo," Noni said, prying her apart from Asha. Once Noni had her attention, she continued, "I love you, girl. Like, I really love you like you my other sister. And I don't look at you no different because you white. But you can't expect the same from these streets. Niggas already ain't shit. And they'll think that just because you a white girl, they can take advantage of you. I ain't telling you not to date black dudes, I'm just saying, at least pick one that got more going on than running the streets. You hear me, girl?"

Lo-Lo nodded, and Noni tenderly touched her discolored face, "Now show us where this nigga live, so we can make his face look worse than yours."

After ordering Lance to stay upstairs and watch TV until they returned, the girls got in the Taurus and drove to Kenny-Boy's house.

"Just play the submissive role," Asha told Lo-Lo as they parked down the street. "It take a weak man to hit a woman, so he'll feed right into it."

Lo-Lo looked down. "Maybe we should leave. Because I can just move on and be done with him."

Asha understood she was afraid and took Lo-Lo's hand. "Domestic violence against women is a serious issue, love. And it's gotten worse because we ain't fighting back. These cowards ain't being made to suffer no real consequences. I can't speak for nobody else, but I'd rather be dead before I let a man mistreat me. And because you my sister, when he hit you, it's like he hit me, too. And I ain't going!"

Noni leaned up from the backseat, "Now get your lil' white ass in there so we can fuck this nigga up."

Lo-Lo couldn't help but crack a slight grin, for she knew Noni was dead serious. *What would I do without these girls?*

Lo-Lo thought to herself before she took a deep breath and bravely exited the car.

The twins watched Lo-Lo walk up to a light-blue house, knock on its door and soon be let inside. "After that fumble at White Castle, I say we wipe this nigga down, too," Noni suggested, as she passed the baseball bat up front.

"See, that's how I know you my twin," Asha smiled, accepting the Louisville Slugger. "You be thinking just like me."

When an upstairs light cut out, the twins put on their ski masks and gloves, quietly closed the car doors behind them, and crept to the side of the house, where Lo-Lo left a downstairs window unlocked.

Once in the house, they waited for their eyes to adjust to the darkness before tiptoeing upstairs. Upon reaching the top landing, they heard sexual sounds coming from a nearby room. With the bat in hand as they advanced toward the partially opened door, Asha thought about how they were about to literally catch Kenny-Boy with his pants down.

Before barging into the bedroom, Asha glanced back at Noni to make sure she was ready. Clutching the pistol, Noni nodded for her sister to proceed. Asha kicked the door wide open and entered the room, ready to showcase her batting skills.

Planted behind Lo-Lo, who he had on the bed in a doggystyle position, Kenny-Boy looked over his shoulder in time to see the aluminum bat coming towards him at an unavoidable speed. He hollered out as it made a merciless connection with his lower back.

When he raised his arm in an attempt to block the second blow, Asha broke the bone at the elbow, then laid him down on the bed with a vicious whack across his legs.

As Lo-Lo hurriedly got dressed and Kenny-Boy groaned in agony, Noni located the light switch and flicked it. "Nigga, shut your bitch ass up before I really give you something to cry about. It was all good when you was hitting on a girl. So keep that same energy, with your coward ass."

He tried to offer a lame excuse and Asha cracked him again. "Didn't she just tell you shut the fuck up?"

Noni took one hand off the gun and reached into her pocket, from where she removed her famous set of brass knuckles and tossed them to Lo-Lo. "Fuck that nigga face up. Give him a taste of his own shit."

"Lo-Lo, I'm sorry," Kenny-Boy whimpered. "I was tweaking, baby girl. I promise it won't ever happen again. You know how crazy I am about you for real. Look at me, baby."

When Lo-Lo's head began slowly turning in his direction, Noni jumped up on the bed, stood over Kenny-Boy and shot him in the face. Picturing the man that molested her, the man from White Castle, and the man that beat up her girl, Noni screamed as she emptied the 7-round clip.

With the hammer clicking as she continued to pull the trigger, Asha reached around to gently remove the gun from her sister's hands. Noni was shedding tears when she turned to look down at Asha, who returned her stare with a loving expression, "It's okay, love, I'm not mad at you. I understand. Now come on, we gotta get out of here."

After shaking Lo-Lo out of her shell-shocked state, Asha told her to take them to Kenny-Boy's stash. She led them downstairs to the kitchen, where she pointed toward a 50-pound bag of dry dog food. "It should be in there."

Upon dumping the food out on the floor, they discovered two kilos of cocaine, but no money. Asha looked up at Lo-Lo. "Where he keep the bread at?"

Shaking her head, Lo-Lo shrugged, "I don't know, I thought he would've kept in there, too."

Asha looked around, wanting to extend her search, but knowing it was too risky. And besides, they could wholesale the coke for more money than they'd ever seen.

With the drugs in her jacket as they jogged from the crime scene, Asha told Lo-Lo to drive, as it would be a much better look if they were to encounter a cop car.

Before tucking herself in the Taurus, Asha listened to her intuition and dropped the murder weapon down a drainpipe.

While quietly en route to their residence, Asha turned to address Noni, who sat in the middle of the backseat. "Where you at, love?" She asked in reference to Noni's mind state. There was a big difference between taking cars and taking a life. And this was Noni's first kill.

Noni looked up, eyes glazed with fulfillment. "Twin, I felt so alive when I was pulling that trigger. It's like I felt a release. And I knew in that moment, no nigga on earth will ever hurt us again. Am I wrong for feeling like that?"

Asha shook her head, "Nah, not at all. I mean, it would be wrong to kill somebody innocent. But any man who hurt a girl deserves to be shot down like the dog he is. So fuck Kenny-Boy, and whoever—"

"Oh my God! Oh my God!" Lo-Lo cried in panic. "Fuck!"

Asha whirled to face her. "What is it?"

As Lo-Lo nervously explained she'd just run a red light, a cop car made a U-turn, activated its sirens and accelerated in their direction. It was instant chaos inside the car. Noni kept turning to stare through the back windshield, swearing she was going to be spending the rest of her life in prison. Lo-Lo was rambling nonstop, thinking about her little brother and what she should do next. And Asha - who was grateful for disposing of the murder weapon - was thinking about the cocaine in her coat. It was an ugly situation, and her usually clever mind was struggling to cook up a fixable remedy.

"Pull over," Asha suddenly announced, praying she was making the right decision.

"What?" Lo-Lo and Noni both exclaimed.

"Just pull over," she repeated. "It might not be nothing but a traffic stop for you running that light. But if we try to outrun 'em and end up getting caught, it's gon' make it look like we got more to hide. Now, just pull over."

A lone officer conducted the stop. Cautiously approaching the car, he asked Lo-Lo for a license she didn't have, while sensing something was faulty inside the Ford. He instructed the driver to turn off the ignition, then ordered everyone to keep their hands in plain sight.

As the officer stepped back from the car and radioed for backup, Asha gave quiet counsel to Lo-Lo and Noni. "Our story simple. We get paid to haul shit. We don't know what it is, or who it belongs to. And we can't say where it comes from, for fear of being killed. That's our story and we sticking to it."

The two kilos were discovered in the glovebox, and the girls were arrested and charged with felony drug possession. But on account of sticking to their stories of being 17-year-old mules, they were never tied to Kenny-Boy's murder, and would ultimately be sentenced to under two years in juvenile prison. The fish can't get caught if it don't open its mouth.

For the sake of Lo-Lo's safety and well-being, the twins had agreed that the murder was worth it. And Noni said she had only one regret in regard to Kenny-Boy's murder - that she her gun didn't hold more than seven bullets. "Like Asha said, I'd rather be dead than let a man mistreat us."

Chapter 11

"How long you gon' keep treating Noni like she an outcast?" Shawna asked Asha from the passenger seat of a Lexus sedan as it moved through traffic. "I can see she hurting, and it's bothering me, Asha."

With Polaris strapped in a car-seat behind them, it was Monday morning, and the girls were en route to PNC for the drop off of their alleged weekend earnings.

"I hear you, Shawna, I really do," Asha replied, steering with just her small left hand. "But I'm still upset with that girl. I just can't stop thinking that if she wouldn't have convinced me to go against my gut feeling, that that D-A-U-R-A situation would've went different. Because who's to say I wouldn't have gotten there in time."

"And whose to say you would've," Shawna countered. "I understand how you feel, because ain't nothing like the feeling of regret. But you acting like life don't happen. Like we immune to certain stuff. And I don't claim to know a whole lot, but I do know that when it's somebody's time to go, it ain't nothing you, me, or nobody else can do to stop it. You my big sis' and I love you to death. But I gotta tell you, if you got beef with Noni, then you got beef with God, too. Because can't nothing happen without Him allowing it. And I don't know if that's some beef you wanna cook up."

Asha frowned at her failure to come up with a rational defense. And as badly as she wanted to rebel, she knew Shawna was right. But that didn't mean she couldn't give her a hard time for it. "So when did you become Dr. Phil's assistant? Ms. "I don't claim to know a whole lot". You couldn't wait to get me alone and go in on me."

Shawna bursted out in laughter. "Oh, no you just didn't! You really gon' try to hit me with that? Girl, if you don't shut your stubborn butt up and tell Noni you sorry. Let you not do it when we get back and see if I don't really go in on you. And you already know how I get down when I get super emotional."

Remembering Shawna's meltdown in Flint, Asha laughingly replied, "Yeah, I definitely don't need you mobbing through the MGM, crying and shit. Them people gon' call security and have us thrown out like the Flintstones."

As the laughing pair pulled into the bank, a tinted SRT Durango followed suit. Inside the black sports utility vehicle was CJ, Double-O, and two hired hounds who held high powered rifles.

CJ smirked as Asha exited the car, carrying a designer handbag. "That girl a gangsta," he praised while watching her walk into the bank. "She literally dropping off drug money in that bitch."

Double-O shot CJ a disapproving glance, which he noticed and awkwardly grinned, "What, bro?"

Postponing his response, Double-O returned his attention to the bank. But he was highly disappointed in his comrade for making such a comment in front of company and would later reprove him in private. He just hoped CJ would be receptive to the counsel and promise to be more conscious of his conduct.

Inside the Lexus sedan, Shawna patted her knee in synch with a Beyoncé song, when she was startled by Polaris calling her name. She quickly lowered the music and turned in her seat, "Yes, baby?"

Since being in their care the little girl had rarely spoken and would usually only do so if the conversation was initiated. And even then, her responses were brief and barely above a whisper. So to hear her speak first made Shawna feel a mixture of nervousness and excitement.

Peering at Shawna through eyes that would've melted the heart of Adolf Hitler, Polaris asked her in the sweetest and sincerest voice, "Are you gon' be my new mama?"

Shawna was speechless. This was nowhere near what she expected to hear. But as she could see that Polaris awaited an answer, she managed to plainly reply, "Polaris, sweetie, you already have a Mama."

The little girl looked down at her lap. "Yeah, but she in heaven, and I'm not. She went without me."

Not knowing what to say in response, Shawna's vision grew blurry from the formation of tears. *Lord, what is this child trying to do to me?* She inwardly prayed, pained by the sight of the little girl's sadness.

Shawna saw Asha returning to the car and quickly wiped her eyes. She wanted to wait until they were alone before bringing up the conversation between her and Polaris.

Grinning as she entered the car, Asha was on the verge of voicing her joy over the balance of their bank account, when she instantly sensed a change in Shawna's energy. And the girl was gazing out the window like she was purposely avoiding eye contact. Unsure of what could've happened in such a short period of time, Asha looked over her shoulder at Polaris, whose attention was focused on the screen of her iPad. Asha turned back to Shawna, observed her for a minute, then decided it was something she'd dig into later and drove off.

Several blocks from the bank Asha pulled into a McDonald's. "You want me to go through the drive-thru, or you want to go inside and eat?" She asked Polaris.

As if weighing her options, she was quiet for a minute before looking up from her iPad and softly speaking, "I wanna go inside."

After nibbling on her nuggets and taking a sip of her chocolate milkshake, Polaris asked Shawna if she could join the other children in the play area.

Shawna looked at Asha, who shrugged in consent, then granted Polaris permission under one condition, "Stay where we can see you."

They were watching her shyly interact with the other children, when Asha commented, "She definitely doing a lot better. And if I had to guess, I'd say it was all because of you."

Shawna eyed her with a doubtful expression, to which Asha assured, "Nah, for real. Your patience with that little girl is exceptional. I mean, you'll literally beg her to eat. You're right there to hold her and console her every time she has a nightmare. And you're so protective of her that, even though she's just a child, she can feel how genuine your love is."

Asha ran a hand of affection over Shawna's hair. "And you wanna know how I know I'm right?"

"How?" She eagerly asked, her child-like eyes gleaming with curiosity. While didn't know it would grow to the extent that it did, Shawna's love for that little girl is what woke her up every morning. She loved Polaris more than anything she had ever loved in her entire life. And in spite of the child's trauma, she was selfishly desperate for the reciprocation of the little girl's love.

"Remember when she asked to go play?" Asha pointed out to Shawna. "She didn't ask Auntie Asha, she asked you. And that just shows she's established a motherly connection with you. She identifies your love and affection with motherhood."

Shawna was so touched by the comment that she brought up the conversation between her and Polaris. "You know it's crazy you say that, because when you went in the bank, I was listening to the music, and I heard Polaris calling my name.

And, Asha, when I turned around and looked at that baby, do you know what she asked me?"

"What, love?" Asha tenderly replied, as she now understood the change in Shawna's energy earlier.

"She asked me if I was gon' be her new mama. And I didn't know what to say, other than she already had a mama. And then she said her mama went to heaven without her, and I thought my heart would come out my body right there in that car. Asha, that baby suffering more than what we know. And I can relate so much, but –"

Asha wiped the falling tears from Shawna's eyes. "And that's why it's gone be okay now, love. Because with someone you like you in her life, she won't be suffering much longer. You gone wrap her up in all that love you got inside you, and she's gone be just fine."

"But what if I fail her, Asha? What if I ain't good enough?"

"Shawna, I don't know if there's another human being on earth with a heart as pure and loving as yours. I ain't the spiritual type, but there ain't no doubt in my mind that God see to it that you a good ass mother. And like I said, you got too much love in you not to be."

Taken as a sign that her prediction was on point, Asha glanced toward the play area and saw Polaris staring in their direction. Asha didn't have the ability to read the little girl's thoughts, but she did have the eyesight to see that she was looking directly at Shawna; as if extending a silent invitation to come play with her.

Bumping Shawna with her elbow, Asha nudged her head toward the play area. "Look. She wants you to come play with her. Now go wrap that baby up in some of that love."

Asha's heart was filled with warmth as she witnessed the playful interaction between Shawna and Polaris. They were what each other needed. And while Asha would forever mourn over the loss of D'Aura, she found a sense of comfort in knowing that on the opposite end of that loss was a much-needed gain for Shawna.

It was a subject too sensitive to regularly discuss, but Asha was aware of Shawna's inability to bear children of her own. Although it resulted from her being repeatedly raped at a young age, Shawna had once cried her heart out to Asha; confessing how worthless she felt as a woman, and how every bad thing that happened to her was somehow her fault.

Asha had held her and cried along with her, saying everything she could think of to convince Shawna otherwise. But without being able to point out Shawna's purpose in life, her encouragement had carried very little weight. So to now see the joyful effects that parenthood was having on Shawna, Asha would unselfishly search for a way to separate Shawna from the Butterfly Mafia. She would always be one of their four wings, just from a safe distance.

As Asha fondly observed Shawna chasing after a giggling Polaris, she realized this was the first time she'd heard the child laugh in a long while. Taking a sip of Polaris' chocolate milkshake, she felt her heartbeat quicken with excitement over the sudden realization of how she could ensure Shawna's safety. "I might've just figured out her purpose," she beamed to herself, while pulling up Google on her pink iPhone.

***

"Noni, protect yourself, got-damit!" Her coach, Andy Bell, yelled from outside the boxing ring. Sparring with a boy who outweighed her by twenty pounds, Noni was pinned against the ropes, doing little to dodge shots that normally wouldn't touch her. She was wonderful with her weave-game, so her coach couldn't comprehend the amount of contact she was absorbing. Something wasn't right, but he'd give it a minute and see how it played out.

Aside from wearing his predominantly gray hair in a ponytail, the 49-year-old Andy Bell constantly wore a stern expression. He was small in stature, large in heart, and humble enough to lend his legendary coaching ability to at-risk kids, free of charge.

Halfway through the following round, Andy Bell saw enough and called it quits. Something was definitely wrong with his fighter and he intended to identify its source. "That's enough for today!" He called out.

After attending the Terrence Crawford fight in Vegas, Noni returned to gym and informed her coach of her desire to go pro. He didn't know what had revived her spirit, but he knew she had what it took to be a world champion. Warning her it would require extreme self-discipline and dedication, he then promised she could punish the present belt-holder of the lightweight division. But after witnessing the poor performance of her latest sparring match, he wondered if he had spoken too soon.

"Noni, you gotta tell me something," Andy Bell said once she removed her headgear and gloves. "Because that shit I just saw in there..." He pointed at the ring, shaking his head in displeasure. "That wasn't it."

She averted her gaze and shrugged, "I don't know what you want me to tell you."

"You can start by telling me the truth! And look at me when I'm talking to you, Noni. I know I at least deserve that much respect from you."

When she reestablished eye contact with a loud sigh, Andy Bell continued, "Listen, if you wanna waste your time, that's on you. But don't carry your ass up in here and waste mines. Look around, you ain't the only fighter in here. But on account of how gifted you are, I put you before everybody else, when I know it's unfair to others. And this how you gone repay me, with some old weak ass sparring?"

"Maybe I am wasting your time, if you gone act like this over me having one bad day."

"A bad day?" Andy repeated as if she couldn't be serious. "Noni, that wasn't a bad day, that was some bullshit. You was letting that boy hit you with shots I know you can slip with your eyes closed. At one point, it seemed like you were letting him hit you on purpose. Like you wanted—"

There was a reactive flash in Noni's eyes that told Andy Bell he was on to something. He slightly tilted his head and regarded Noni with a searching expression. "You wanted him to hit you, didn't you? You let him do it on purpose. What's going on with you, Noni?"

As tears welled up in her eyes in response, he felt his heart go out to her, for Noni had shown emotion in front of him. Whatever was troubling her, he knew it must've weighed a substantial amount.

"Listen, whatever it is, I won't push you to talk about it," he said in an empathetic tone. "I mean, I'm here if you ever need a listening ear, and I understand if you don't. But let me leave you with something before you go. Noni, you special. You gotta gift that can only be God-given. And just like God didn't make a bunch of Terrence Crawford's or Floyd Mayweather's, neither did he make a bunch of Noni Kincaid's. So take advantage of what you've been given, before it's too late. Do you know how many people live and die like they were never even here? Like they never existed? But you gotta chance to make a difference, to actually leave something behind. You don't wanna get to the end, look back and there's nothing to see, Noni. Because I promise you, the graveyard is packed with regretful people."

Inside a small locker room that was just for her, Noni sat on a bench with her head down. On the floor, between her crisp Air Jordan's, were a collection of teardrops. Noni was in pain. And it had nothing to do with the intentional beating she took in the ring, but from the guilt she felt over causing Asha heartache. Her better half hated her, and Noni didn't know how to fix it. She'd become so emotionally dependent on Asha, that she found it too tough to function without her twin's love and affection.

"I fucked up bad," Noni sadly admitted to herself. "And maybe I'd be better off not here no more."

Chapter 12

IMAX State Prison

Upon Kavoni McClain being admitted into the visiting room, it was as if someone pressed pause on all interactions. And it wasn't the fact that his features were undoubtedly handsome, or that his prison garb did little to disguise a muscular structure emblazoned with ink. But it was his authoritative aura, which emitted the scent of a savage and the polish of a patriarch.

As he crossed the room in low white Forces, Kavoni could relate to the iconic Tupac, as all eyes were literally on him. And though he maintained a stoic expression along his march, he had to admit that it felt damn good to be attentively observed by outside civilians.

When his visitor rose to greet him as he approached the table, Kavoni was honestly impressed by her womanly appearance. With her hair and make-up done to perfection, she rocked a pink hoodie over matching Dior sneakers.

"Look at my lil' sister!" He exclaimed, as him and Shawna embraced like long lost relatives, which in a sense they were. "It's so good to see you, my baby!"

"It's good to see you, too," Shawna beamed, truly enraptured by their reunion. Besides Double-O and Martha, Kavoni was the closest thing she had to her late friend, Puma.

They disengaged and he held her at arm's length. "I can't believe how mature you look. Puma would be so proud of you."

His praise caused Shawna to lower her head, as she recalled past behaviors that would've disappointed Puma. But history was something you couldn't rewrite; you could only move forward and modify your narrative.

"Damn, girl, is there anything you didn't get?" Kavoni teased her as they took a seat, referring to a table full of snacks and soft drinks.

Shawna grinned, "I didn't know what you liked, so I just got some of everything."

Pleased with her logic, he offered his gratitude before reaching for a bottle of Pepsi. It was somewhat sad how the simplest things in life could mean the most to an inmate - one such as sipping an ice cold soda.

"Kavoni, I know we haven't seen each other in a while," Shawna said with a straight face, "But I was wondering if you could send me a ticket?"

He frowned in confusion. "A ticket? A ticket for what?"

"For the gun show!" She pointed at his biceps and bursted out in laughter, prompting the killer to join in with her.

"Girl, that was corny as hell," he smiled, "But it's good to see you not all shy no more. I remember you would barely talk, let alone tell a joke."

It had been nearly five years since Kavoni had last saw Shawna. And from he recalled, she was a timid young girl who would avoid eye contact. So it was refreshing to see that she had built up her confidence.

"So, what's been going on with you? What you been up to?" Kavoni inquired.

"Just taking it one step at a time. Trying to find my path, you know?"

Kavoni nodded, "Just keep searching and you'll find it. We all got one, whether its found or not. But I can tell you this, when you go through a lot in life, but you keep waking up every day, then that just means that your purpose hasn't been fulfilled yet. So don't ever think you're not here for a reason."

As Shawna considered his encouragement with a thoughtful expression, he asked her if she had brought any money, which she said she did. "Alright, come on, let's go take some pictures," he suggested.

After posing for a pair of photographs and returning to the table, Kavoni opened a bag of Flamin' Hot Cheetos and popped several in his mouth. "So wassup with your lil' crew?" He casually asked. "Everybody well?"

"My crew?" A surprised Shawna repeated, thinking Double-O must've ran his mouth. "How you know about my crew?"

"Just because I'm locked up don't mean I'm not in tune. I probably know more about what's going in the streets than most of the niggas who actually out there. And besides, a deaf mu'fucka could hear all the noise the Butterfly Mafia making. But let me ask you, Shawna, is every girl in your crew worthy of being trusted?"

Shawna thought about Lo-Lo's love affair before nodding, "Yeah, I trust every one of them. They embraced me when I was at my lowest. And they never once judged me. Other than Puma, they're the only girls who ever looked out for me and accepted me for who I am. So yeah, I trust them with my life, and I love them all like they're my real sisters."

From the sincerity in her eyes to the passion in her voice, Kavoni knew she had genuine love for her crew. And he wouldn't attempt to plant seeds of mistrust in her mind, but he would encourage her to always be watchful of the signs. "On account of Puma, I look at you like my little sister. So I want what's best for you. And since I'm not physically able to be part of your journey, I can only give you what I've learned through experience and hope it'll help you in whatever direction you're headed. I know for a fact you got a good heart, or Puma wouldn't have kept you around. But, Shawna, don't let kindness be your killer."

"What does that mean?" She earnestly asked.

"Kindness can impair your judgement. It can prevent you from making certain decisions, out of concern for someone else's feelings. When in all actuality, you can't save nobody else until you save yourself. But sometimes we can be so considerate of others that we lose sight of who matters the most - which is ourselves. And that's how kindness can end up being your killer."

Shawna was appreciative of his counsel - which she would definitely keep in mind, but she was more curious about Kavoni's situation. The man was sentenced to life without parole, a reality that surely deprived him of sleep on many nights. "If you don't want to talk about it, I understand, but what is it like here for you? Like, how do you stop from going insane? I did a few months in juvie, but I can't imagine being in here for years."

It wasn't done consciously, but Kavoni's chin slightly lifted in a gesture of strength before he answered, "This shit madness for real, but I embrace it with a smile. When you sign to the streets, you gotta accept what comes with it, whether you want to or not. And as far as my day-to-day, I work out like a marine and do mass reading."

"Oh, yeah, like what?" Shawna smiled.

"For a minute I was caught up in them hood books, because I could relate to a lot of the stories. It's a company called Lock Down Publications, and a bunch of they joints be floating around. But lately I've been reading more self-help books, shit that help build character. If I'ma see the streets again, I gotta be prepared to put on a different uniform and perform for a whole different crowd, you feel me. A nigga can't give back an elbow and go right back to the same shit. I might as well stay in here and let somebody else take my place."

"What's an elbow?" Shawna asked.

Kavoni smiled at her curious nature. "That's what we call a life sentence. They'll either say a nigga gotta 'L', or a 'elbow'. So what else you wanna know? Because I really don't like dwelling on this jail shit for real."

"Yeah, I understand. I was just curious, that's all."

"Listen to me, my baby," he eyed her closely, deciding it was best to put her mind at ease. "I speak for all the real ones when I say there's no such thing as too much pressure. Ain't no breaking point for a gangsta. You either built for this shit, or you ain't. Regardless of his environment, a man gone either move like a King or a clown. Prison just happens to be a place where it strip a nigga of everything but his character. Ain't no cars, clothes, or jewelry to make a man appear to be more than what he really is. So it's plenty of niggas who get exposed in this bitch, whether it's them turning out to be mentally weak or hoes at heart. But when you lay down and go to sleep at night, the last thing you gotta worry about is Kavoni McClain not to going to his grave as a cold gangsta. Ain't no fold in me, my baby. So whether it's in heaven or hell, I'ma hold it down, you hear me?"

Believing every syllable he spoke, Shawna was momentarily silent at the intensity of his delivery. He had the heart of a warrior and she admired him for it.

Now came the hard part. And with neither of them wanting to approach the subject, it was Shawna who dove headfirst into the past and caused a splash of painful memories. "Double-O don't really like talking about it, but he told me what really happened with Puma."

In addition to several other slayings he didn't commit, Kavoni was charged and convicted for the murder of his best friend, Puma. He'd repeatedly told his lawyers he was being set up, but with her body found in his trunk, along with the murder weapons, he had a better chance at convincing Kevin Hart that he wasn't done growing.

"Yeah, it was Mecca," Kavoni confirmed, bitterly recalling a woman he once loved. "She was rocking me to sleep the entire time. That shit was so shrewd, it made me reevaluate my whole... everything. Because yo, I swear I didn't even know I was being rocked until I woke the fuck up."

Kavoni went on to reveal how Mecca's motive had been revenge for the murder of her younger sister. And as his level of reasoning rose over the years, he understood his current circumstances to be the reaping result of bad karma. He had killed the young girl in cold blood; a merciless act that came with a punishment as stiff as her corpse - being buried alive. However, that didn't diminish his desire to plant Mecca right alongside her sibling. While Kavoni's belief was that there were no stipulations on street-level revenge, Mecca had robbed him of too much to simply excuse. And he vowed to get even if ever released.

"Wow, bro, that's crazy," Shawna slowly shook her head. "But you know what's even crazier? I actually saw her a few weeks ago."

Kavoni flew forward and frowned. "Where?"

"At a funeral in Flint. And once I told Double-O, he was super mad. He said he would've killed her right there in that church."

Kavoni dreamed of revenge, but not at the expense of Double-O's freedom. So he was grateful for the missed opportunity of him killing her in public. And he also understood Double-O's reason for not mentioning that Mecca had been recently spotted. Double-O was a man of action, who wouldn't waste words until the war was won.

Looking over his shoulder as a guard announced visits were over, Kavoni turned back to Shawna. "Do you remember the last time we talked?" He asked in a hurried tone, to which she nodded. "Well, I never got the chance to talk to you again after that day," he continued. "And the not knowing ate at me all the way up until Double-O told me he met you. I say that to say this, Shawna, I don't ever wanna experience that feeling again. So I don't want you involved with that Mecca situation. That woman wicked."

"Visiting hours are over, McClain," a guard walked up, handing him the two pictures him and Shawna had taken. "So tell your little girlfriend adios and let's go."

"This my baby sister," Kavoni corrected him with a murderous glare.

"Yeah, well, like I said," the guard withered under the inmate's stare, "Visiting hours are over."

Repressing the urge to catch an assault charge, Kavoni gave Shawna a picture, gathered her in his arms and squeezed her. "Be good, my baby, and don't stop searching till you find it. Now go embrace who you are as a young lioness, and I'll see you on the other side."

Without giving Shawna a chance to reply, Kavoni abruptly withdrew from the embrace and turned to walk off.

Confused by his cold departure, Shawna watched as he exited the visiting room without once looking back. *What the hell just happened?* She wondered, willing herself not to resort to what she did best.

Walking across the prison's parking lot, contemplating the reason for Kavoni's strange behavior, Shawna approached the passenger side of a Nissan coupe and got inside.

Double-O paused on pulling off as he noticed her troubled expression. "Aye, yo, you good?" He curiously inquired. Agreeing to bring Shawna to see Kavoni after the recent termination of her probation, Double-O had camped out in the parking lot during their two-hour reunion.

Shawna's voice cracked as she answered, "I don't know. I mean, everything was all good one minute, then at the end of the visit he told me he'd see me on the other side and just walked off. He didn't even give me a chance to say goodbye, or nothing."

They sat in silence for a minute before she turned to Double-O with glossy eyes. "It's me, ain't it? He didn't want to see me. He blame me for what happened to Puma, don't he?"

Double-O shook his head, to which Shawna asked, "Then, why would he act like that?"

He thought of how to best explain it and settled on simply serving her the truth. "Kavoni wanted to see you as much as you wanted to see him, trust me. But I already knew it would be hard for him the end, you know, the seeing you leave part. You gotta understand, Kavoni a protector by nature. That's his strength, that's what gives him a sense of purpose. And seeing you in person was like sitting across from Puma. And right now he not in a position to protect you for real, which just reminds him of how he wasn't there to protect Puma, either. So it ain't personal against you, it's just shit he battling with on the inside. Not to mention he is fighting for his freedom. But when he said he'll see you on the other side, you best believe that day on the way. They don't make too many like Kavoni, so I already know this ain't how his story gone end."

Chapter 13

The Butterfly Mafia were gathered in the front room of their MGM suite. Holding Polaris on her lap, Shawna had the floor as she gave a recap of her visit with Kavoni. "And I swear he built like an action figure, y'all. When I hugged him it was like gripping a statue. That's how solid he felt, like stone."

From the ages of six to sixty, there wasn't a citizen in the city who hadn't mentioned the name Kavoni McClain. His former crew, The N.F.L. were dubbed the most dangerous Detroit had ever seen. Widely known for the monstrous means of his meteoric rise to riches, Kavoni had once beheaded a man who'd ran off on the plug and returned the drugs to their rightful owner; thus earning him a seat at a kingpin's table. A short-haired hoodlum who was handsome and heartless, Kavoni was an idol even rivals respected. And he just so happened to be Shawna's big brother, which had the girl's all ears as she vocally relived their reunion.

"Oh damn, I almost forgot," Shawna leaned over to reach in her purse. She withdrew the picture of her and Kavoni and handed it to Asha. "That's him right there."

As the picture was passed between the three girls, their study of it led to similar conclusions - the man had the glow of an Egyptian god, with the devilish dark eyes of Satan's firstborn.

"So when you going to see him again?" Lo-Lo asked as she handed the picture back to Shawna.

Her brightness dimmed at the inquiry. "I'm not."

Asha's head tilted in curiosity. "Why is that?"

"He told me he'd see me on the other side. At first I was lost. Then Double-O explained that him seeing me in person is too painful for him. I remind him of Puma too much, and right now that ain't good for his mental health. I thought about it on the ride back, and I understand. He couldn't protect Puma back then, and he feel like he can't protect me now. So seeing my face is like a physical reflection of his failures. But as long as I can talk to him on the phone, I'm good with that."

As Shawna repeated what Kavoni had said about his spirit being unbreakable, Asha caught eyes with her twin and slipped her a wink; which warmed Noni's heart to a euphoric degree.

Right after receiving Shawna's tongue lashing, Asha pulled her sister aside and apologized for her mean behavior. Eager to accept the heartfelt apology, Noni, too, apologized and swore to never again second guess Asha's intuition. Along with an exchange of 'I love yous', the twins buried the past with a lengthy hug.

While Noni was unaware of what motivated Asha's apology, she did know that its timeliness likely saved her life. She was neither proud nor ashamed of having suicidal thoughts, but the sadness of feeling unworthy was real. Sure, there were some who'd associate weakness with her seeking validation from her sibling, but Asha had replaced the role of Regina and raised her with the closest emotion to a mother's love. So not only was Noni eternally grateful for Asha's devotion, but she had long ago settled she'd sacrifice her life for the sake of saving her beloved sister's.

"So, what did he say when you told him how much money you put on his books?" Asha asked Shawna to lighten the mood.

Shawna flashed a mischievous grin. "I didn't tell him, on purpose. I can't wait till he see it and call me."

Prior to her visit with Kavoni, Shawna and the girls had discussed the idea of blessing their elder with a decent donation. In light of his honorable character - for which Shawna and the streets could personally vouch, it was a collective decision to deposit five grand into his prison account.

"And what was you and Double-O talking about for all them hours y'all was riding in that car?" Lo-Lo questioned in a teasing tone. "I know y'all ain't just listen to music the whole time."

"Lo-Lo!" Shawna blushed in embarrassment. "Me and Double-O just friends, it ain't nothing like that."

"Mm, hmm," Lo-Lo skeptically replied. "I see the way he be watching you when he don't think nobody looking.

"Asha, do you hear this?" Shawna sought her assistance.

She held up her hands as a gesture of being neutral.

Shawna then turned to Noni, who also threw up her hands and laughingly stated, "My name Bennet and I ain't in it."

"It's okay, Shawna," Lo-Lo smiled, "You ain't gotta keep it a secret, we ain't gone judge you."

"That's because ain't nothing to judge or no secret to keep."

Lo-Lo began singing, "Shawna and Double-O sitting in a tree, k-i-s-s-i-"

Shawna covered Polaris' ears. "Don't listen to her, baby. She being a bad auntie."

As the girls joined in laughter, Asha was thinking how Lo-Lo was right in regard to how Double-O looked at Shawna. That was her real reason for staying neutral; as she didn't want to lie, or cause Shawna further embarrassment by admitting the truth.

***

Having snuck out the hotel, Lo-Lo lied in the backseat of the Denali, FaceTiming with Uno. "I miss you, too, baby," she beamed at the screen of her iPhone.

"Shit, I can't tell," Uno replied, "I ain't seen you in days, and you been acting really strange. I'm starting to think you giving that candy to somebody else."

"Nah, never that. It's just been a lot going on, and I gotta be supportive of my girls."

"That's what you keep saying, Lo-Lo, but that shit getting old. I'm saying, I ain't never been on no thirsty shit. So I don't know if you got me mistaken, or what. But all this secretive shit, like you gotta sneak around to kick it, I ain't feeling it, my baby. So either meet me in the middle, or let's just move around."

Lo-Lo looked up from the phone and sighed in frustration. She was frustrated at Uno for being willing to give up. Frustrated at Asha for being so damn paranoid. And frustrated at the fact that Uno had a right to feel how he felt. In spite of wanting to scream, Lo-Lo returned her attention to the screen and surrendered to vulnerability.

"Uno, baby, I need you to really listen to me. Baby, I care about you in a way I've never cared for no other man. Like, me being honest, you're literally my first thought in the morning and my last one at night. Whenever I'm with you, I feel safe, I feel a sense of security. And that's not something I got from my own father. So I don't expect you to fully understand how attached to you I've gotten. So if you could just understand I'm in a stressful situation. It's like, my loyalty to my girls pulling one arm, and my love for you pulling the other. Right now I don't know what to do, but I do know I don't want you to stop pulling."

As he saw the sincerity in her pleading blue eyes, Uno couldn't deny the heartwarming effects of her emotional spiel. And not only were his feelings equally intense, but he could also relate to the wearisome tug-of-war between love and loyalty.

"If you really don't want a nigga to stop pulling, then I'ma need you to make that happen."

Lo-Lo was lost. "Make what happen?"

"Shit, a nigga ain't had no candy in a minute. I'm over this bitch with a sweet tooth like a mu'fucka."

Lo-Lo considered it but quickly dismissed it. "Uno, not tonight, baby, I'm sorry. For one, I'm way out. And two, I'm babysitting a 5-year-old."

"Well, shoot me the addy and I'm on my way right now."

"Boy, my girl would kill me if I gave out her address. My own little brother don't know where she live."

"There you go with all this secretive shit again."

"Uno, I ain't –" Lo-Lo gasped at an image that suddenly appeared on his phone.

"You see this nigga?" Uno demanded, as he showed her his throbbing erection. "Explain that shit to him, Lo'. Explain to him why you got him on punishment."

"Oh my god," she groaned in thirst of the mouthwatering image. "Why he look so angry, baby?"

"Because he is, got-damit! You keep holding that lil' shit hostage."

At the thought of the orgasmic high his pipe could provide, Lo-Lo's hand unconsciously crept between her thighs. "Uno, please put him up," she whimpered in withdrawal, squirming like an addict in need of a fix.

"Nah, you need to see this," he showed his erection from various angles. "Look!" He pointed out pre-cum that appeared at the tip. "You got him over here crying and shit."

With her lonely yoni leaking tears of its own, Lo-Lo looked at his limb and lewdly admitted, "I just wanna put him in my mouth and suck every tear out them big ass balls."

The penis jerked as if it had ears.

"Damn, you'll suck this mu'fucka like that?"

"Even better," she licked her lips. "All neck, no hands."

"I wanna stare into your blue-ass eyes while you eat this mu'fucka on the slow side."

"Baby, I'll eat that big dick like my life literally depend on it. And to make sure I do it right, you can wrap your hands in my hair and move my head at your will."

"Well, since I can't get that pussy in person, I'ma need you to get it for me," Uno said, beginning to strip off all his clothes.

"How I'ma do that?"

"You can start by taking off them panties."

But, Uno, I'm outside in the -"

"Bitch, I said take them muthafuckas off!"

To Lo-Lo's surprise, being called out her name made her yoni get wetter and her nipples even harder.

With her heartbeat pounding as she submissively complied, she eagerly awaited his next instruction.

"Is it wet?" He asks, slowly stroking himself.

"Yes, daddy."

"Let me hear it."

Placing the phone just inches from her vulva, she inserted a finger and stirred it.

"Like macaroni," he pleasurably sighed, referring to the squishy-like sounds. "Now put another finger in there."

"Uno!" She moaned from the addition of her middle finger. "Oh my god, daddy, I don't think I've ever been this wet."

Now stroking himself at a faster pace, he ordered the insertion of a third finger. "Play with that muthafucka, Lo'. Dig up in there like it's this dick. Make that pussy come all over my shit!"

The more he encouraged her the deeper she dug and the louder she moaned. "Daddy, I'ma come all over that big dick!"

"Whose pussy you playing with?"

"It's yours, daddy!"

"Whose white bitch is you?"

"I'm your white bitch!"

"Well, make me know it and make that pussy come."

She turned her attention to her throbbing clitoris and rapidly flicked it. "Daddyyy!"

"Get it, bitch. Get that pussy."

When she felt the familiar sensations of an oncoming orgasm, she urged him to join her on the journey. "Daddy, I'm about to come. I want you to -"

There was a startling knock on the window of the truck and Lo-Lo dropped the phone.

"Are you okay in there?" A male's voice asked from the truck's passenger side.

She quickly pulled up her panties before answering that everything was fine. "I'm just on the phone with my boyfriend."

"OK, ma'am, I'm sorry if I startled you. I was just doing my rounds and heard all the noise."

Shit! She cursed to herself, deciding it was best to cure his concern. The last thing she needed was for him to summon the cops.

Adjusting her clothes, she ran a hand through her hair and went to assure him she wasn't in danger. But as she reached for the door handle, she noticed the guard chuckling to himself as he walked off. Her late-night affair was nothing new to his ears.

"Damn, girl, what the fuck happened?" Uno asked as she reappeared on the screen.

"Boy, you had me over here making all that noise, and the security guard heard me. His freaky ass was probably beating the hell out that lil' Mexican dick."

"Yeah, fuck all that," Uno waved his hand. "Bitch, pull them panties back down so I can bust this nut."

Sexually aroused by Uno's aggression, she obediently removed her panties and their session resumed.

Chapter 14

Solo in his Nissan as he sped through the D, Double-O was on a call with Kavoni. They were discussing Mecca's recent sighting. "I just wish Shawna could've told me sooner," he squeezed the wheel in soundless fury. "Because that bitch would've been buried by now, bro."

"Nah, you might've moved reckless, my baby," Kavoni sensibly replied. "And the last thing I need is for us to be bunkies. You one of the only people out there I can trust, so I need you to stay calm and careful."

"I hear you, bro."

"Some soldiers not expendable, 'O. Always remember that. And as far as that snake... when we track it down, we gone make us some boots."

Bobbing his head with a maniacal smile, Double-O could envision the tortuous event. He had never been a fan of harming a woman, but Mecca was an exception he was willing to make.

"And I'm thinking you might wanna slide through Flint on the quiet side," Kavoni continued. "Just to see what you can learn about the dead, you feel me. Because the snake was either at that funeral to see a friend or a foe. But either way, there's a connection."

Before ending the call, Kavoni restated the importance of Shawna's protection. "Do your absolute best to keep her safe, my baby. Puma would never forgive me."

"I got you, bro," Double-O assured him. "It'll happen to me before it happen to her."

"A'ight, my baby, I'm about to put this joint up," Kavoni said in reference to his prohibited cellphone. "But keep me posted, and be sure to stay dangerous."

"Already," Double-O replied, currently clutching a 30-round cannon.

Besides CJ and his younger cousin, Teer, Kavoni was Double-O's only other comrade. He an army of associates - which was based on business, but those were the only three men he lent his trust. And with Kavoni being the eldest, and the most genuine general he knew, Double-O looked forward to his release from captivity.

Double-O was several blocks from his house, when he saw a lone woman in a red miniskirt. For her to be out in the streets at this time of night could only mean one thing, they were looking for each other.

He slowed the coupe to a coast and lowered his window. "Excuse me, ma'am?"

As if unaccustomed to such courtesy, the woman looked around before pointing at herself, "Who you talking to, me?"

"I apologize if I'm out of pocket. I just thought I could help you help us. But you be safe out here."

Before he could raise his window and roll off, she inquired, "Help me how?"

He brandished a bankroll, to which she replied, "And what all you expect me to do for that?"

"Just some slow oral, if you don't mind."

Double-O didn't know it, but the woman was already familiar with who he was. On account of this being his weekly routine - along with the astounding amounts he'd award the performance, his description had been shared amongst certain solicitors. So when his window had lowered and revealed the curly bush of hair and motor oil complexion, the woman had to refrain from appearing overly excited.

Settling her cinnamon-colored thighs on the Nissan's seats, she smiled at Double-O and showcased a decent set of teeth. "Oh, you even more handsome up close, with your lil' young ass."

He knew she lied about his looks, but he understood. And as he took in the scars on her attractive features, and the experienced brown eyes that shined with struggle, he felt genuine sympathy for someone who was out here simply clawing for survival.

Double-O drove around the corner and reversed the car in between two buildings that sat across from a 7-Eleven. Killing the lights, he scanned the area with a keen eye before blessing his passenger with the bankroll he'd shown her.

She thumbed through it and couldn't help looking over at him. "Baby, not that I ain't grateful as a bitch, but do you know how much this is?"

He nodded, knowing she held nearly a grand in her hand.

His uncommon generosity and well-mannered behavior caused her to give him a closer look. And in doing so, she saw a portrait of pain beyond the windows of his soul. This young boy had been through a lot. And if she wasn't in such desperate need of the money, she would've returned it and performed for free.

"I can tell you've been through a storm or two," she said while securing the funds in her bra, "But I get the feeling brighter days are ahead. So keep it high and tight, and see if the sun don't eventually rise. But until then..." She gathered her hair in a ponytail, "Let me come over there and show you just how grateful I am."

Gripping the steering wheel in one hand and his gun in the other, Double-O fought not to close his eyes as she pleased him with a skill that should've been trademarked.

In midst of him moaning at the tickle of her tongue, he saw something across the street that seized his attention. Halting her head movements with the palm of his hand, he leaned forward to focus on the 7-Eleven's parking lot.

After a minute of being motionless, the woman removed him from her mouth and looked up to see Double-O intensely staring straight ahead. "Is something wrong?" She asked in concern.

When he failed to readily respond, she went to raise up and he held her in place. "Nah, we good. I saw the 'boys' at 7-Eleven, and I was just waiting for them to leave."

Pacified with his answer, she lowered her head and went back to work. But despite her slow tempo and skillful techniques, Double-O was oblivious to the oral activity; for his thoughts were centered on a sudden dilemma.

Meanwhile...

A dark red Charger was parked down the block from the trap house belonging to the Butterfly Mafia. Inside the car were two hooded figures; one a Bandgang member, and the other a traitor the streets knew as CJ.

"...and you saying she gon' shut this bitch down in less than two weeks?" The driver, D-Nutty, said in disbelief, as he witnessed the constant flow of addicts the building attracted. "Bruh, that don't even make sense. Especially not when this bitch jumping like this at one in the morning."

"That's how she been doing it since day one," CJ explained from the passenger seat. "So by the time 'twelve' get hip, she already on the move. Then every nigga she got in there, under eighteen. So if they get knocked, they ain't facing mass time."

Genuinely impressed, D-Nutty nodded his head in recognition of Asha's intellect. "Yeah, that's smart," he admitted. "It cut down on the chances of a nigga telling on her. One of them lil' niggas will go lay it down for a few months in juvie and be right back out."

CJ went on to further explain the means by which Asha stayed ready for a robbery or a raid. As D-Nutty listened to how she arranged daily pick-ups at a various times, and had secret trapdoors built behind refrigerators, he wondered if it was her brain alone that came up with these ingenuous ideas.

"But for real though, I gotta lick way bigger than this building," CJ informed him. "But you gone have to get busy in broad day."

"I don't know, bruh," D-Nutty shook his head in doubt. "They say this building doing like ten bands a day. And from I'm what I'm seeing, shit, it might be more than that."

CJ eyed him as if he was stupid. "Nigga, is you not listening? I just told you she do pick-ups every muthafucking day. So the most you gone get is that lil' ten bands you talking about, and maybe like a brick out the building, if you lucky enough to even get in there. And you saying you content with that?"

D-Nutty didn't like the belittling tone in which CJ had spoken, but for the sake of prosperity he swallowed his pride and calmly answered, "Hell nah, I ain't cool with that. Not if we can get more."

"And I'm telling you we can get more," CJ stamped with conviction. "I'm saying like... two-hundred thousand more."

D-Nutty instantly looked at him, to which CJ confirmed with a nod of his head, "Yeah, you heard me, nigga. Two-hundred thousand. What you think they doing with all this drug money? Every weekend she bring a bag of it to the club and throw it on the white bitch. Then, Monday morning she dropping that shit off at PNC like it's legal. And me and Double-O be following her, with two young niggas in the back that got AR's and shit. So that's why I say you gon' have to get busy."

CJ and D-Nutty were old acquaintances who had pulled off a few capers together in the past. Not knowing D-Nutty already had plans for the Butterfly Mafia, CJ had reached out to him with regard to a robbery. Upon D-Nutty hearing who the intended targets were, he knew this was the window he needed and agreed to climb through before CJ could close it. But he hadn't expected to learn he could come up on

$200,000. A lick like that should be kept under wraps. And in chapter 1 of D-Nutty's handbook, it clearly stated there was only one way for two people to keep a secret— if one of them were dead.

"And you say the two niggas that be with y'all got AR's?" D-Nutty recalled, thinking of the best way to approach the situation.

CJ nodded. "And Double-O make sure they keep both them bitches on ready-to-fire. So, I'm thinking you might have to catch us when we coming out the club that morning. I can shoot you a text and you can already be posted."

Frowning, D-Nutty shook his head at the idea. "Nah, nigga, that might turn into a fire fight. And you just said them lil' niggas got assault rifles and shit. Fuck I'ma do with the money if I'm dead?"

"Then bring backup. Two hunnid enough for you to spread. I just want my half."

Greed made D-Nutty decline. "This solo dolo. If I gotta get busy, I don't need no co-d's."

"Well, the only other thing I can think of is if you catch her at the bank, when she walking in. That's the only time she gon' be alone."

D-Nutty thought for a minute and bobbed his head. "Yeah, that's it. I'll catch her when she get out the car. And it ain't like I'm running up in the bank. We talking about a black bitch with a bag of money. So ain't no way they investigation gon' be that thorough."

"So, you gon' be ready to move in, like, two weeks?" CJ wishfully asked.

D-Nutty eyed him in suspicion and revealed what he was thinking. "I'm saying, bruh, what about Double-O? Ain't that still your main mans?"

"Ain't no mystery. But this ain't got nothing to do with that. This them hoes money, not his."

"So you telling me these bitches ain't feeding y'all? They making all this money, and y'all ain't seeing none of it? Come on, fam'ly."

"Bruh, that nigga Double-O don't see me as no hustler. He got some other niggas selling the weight, while we out here on some Batman and Robin shit. And I'm the fucking sidekick. That nigga might be cool with following these bitches around all day, ready to kill or be killed, but I'm trying to expand, my baby. So I'ma use my half to figure it out. Shit, I might even take my show on the road. I hear it's a sweet as fuck down there in Ohio."

Sensing the truth in CJ's venting, D-Nutty scratched out his suspicion and replaced it with his signature. "A'ight, I'm all in. But this a move we gotta take to our graves."

As they sealed the deal with a handshake, both men were thinking about how this was a secret they'd bury with the other. It would all boil down to whoever drew first.

"I see your boy, Uno, got that white bitch head all fucked up," CJ joked as they drove back to his car. "That bitch beefing with her girls over that nigga."

D-Nutty sourly replied, "Man, fuck that weak ass nigga. I been telling him she a goldmine, and he trying to save the bitch. What real street nigga pick pussy or paper? But fuck it. Now, I'ma just go around his dumb ass." When they pulled up next to CJ's four-door Dodge Ram truck, D-Nutty commented in sarcasm, "You know, for a nigga who allegedly ain't touching no paper, you sure is riding in a big boy Ram. And I know that bitch at least like a fifty-ball."

CJ scoffed. "Nigga, with all the money them hoes making, I supposed to be in a foreign on Forgi's. Fuck you talking 'bout?"

They dapped-up in farewell before CJ got out. As he watched D-Nutty drive off, he was smiling to himself; for he could already picture the paper in his palms.

Upon CJ tucking himself inside the pickup and bringing it to life, the last song he was listening to resumed playing.

"...seem like I lost more than I ever gain/ I ain't get nothing out these streets but pain/ I ain't get nothing out these streets but hard times/ because in these streets ain't nothing but hard times. "

As Kodak Black bared his soul on the song *Versatile*, CJ sped out the 7-Eleven's parking lot with a squeal that scarred the concrete.

Wondering about Double-O's whereabouts as he paused at a light, CJ lowered the music and phoned his friend through the 12-inch screen on his dash. "What the fuck?" He mumbled at the sound of Double-O's ringtone. When he turned toward the source of the sound, CJ flinched as he found himself staring into Double-O's eyes. The man he was calling was seated behind him in the backseat.

CJ attempted to mask his fear with fury. "Damn, bro, what the fuck you doing sitting back there like that? Type of weird shit you on, nigga?"

"I just wanna know why?" Double-O asked with a hurt expression. His inner circle was already the size of a Cheerio. Any smaller would make it a fist.

Knowing Double-O was too shrewd to be fed with lies, CJ figured their friendship would gain him forgiveness and fed him the truth. "Bro, I'm tired of putting my life on the line for peanuts, or for a group of hoes who ain't even old enough to buy their own alcohol. Come on, my baby, we done seen way too much to be settling like this."

"So you thought to approach one of the grimiest niggas in the city before you came to me? Your true comrade? I'm willing to die for you, bro."

As CJ averted his gaze in guilt, he glanced at the center console. Inside was a locked and loaded firearm. "Bro, don't none of this lessen my love for you," he said, casually placing his hand on the console. "But you gotta understand, my loyalty lie with you, not with some bitches I just met last year."

Double-O shook his head in sadness at CJ's logic. "I guess you forgot these the same bitches, as you call 'em, took you from riding a bike to your job at Jiffy Lube. When none of these niggas out here gave you a chance, these girls you just met did. And they did it on the strength of me, and you know where my heart at."

When CJ looked back and saw Double-O had tears coming down his face, he knew it was now or never and quickly opened the console. But before he could get a grip on the gun, Double-O leaned forward and fired a round through his right temple. Despite the splatter of brain matter on the front windshield, Double-O fired four more rounds into his slumped comrade. He was simply ensuring that when paramedics arrived there'd be nothing to revive.

With the truck slowly coasting across the intersection, Double-O threw on his hood, hopped out the Ram and took off running.

It was seeing CJ and D-Nutty link up at 7-Eleven that had actually seized Double-O's attention when he'd been in the car with the woman. He couldn't believe his eyes as he witnessed his friend solidly embrace a known jack-boy— one who just happened to be related to Uno. Hoping CJ could justify his actions with a valid excuse, Double-O was heartbroken as he listened to him admit his hatred for the women who were outright genuine. With a creed of integrity inscribed on his heart, Double-O's only option was to treat him accordingly.

You see, Marjuan McCray would forever be friends with loyalty, even if it meant murdering a man whose death made him cry.

Chapter 16

It felt like an eternity, but the twins' 21st birthday had finally arrived. In celebration of the long-awaited day, they threw a party at Skittles and invited nearly everyone they knew. There was an abundance of catered food and cases of champagne— all of which their guests could consume at no cost. Topped off with the DJ's rotation of hit songs, this would certainly be boasted as the party of the year.

Wearing an off-white sweater over stonewashed jeans and pink-and-white sneakers, Asha exchanged hugs and pleasantries with people in attendance as she made her rounds. She expressed mild surprise at seeing Reverend Daniels, who wore regular clothing. "Hey, Rev'!" She extended her arms for a hug. "I'm glad you could make it."

"I wouldn't have missed it for the world, little sister. But aside from the festivities, how are you?" The Reverend implored, recalling her worried state during their last encounter.

Asha shrugged. "I guess you can say I'm doing better in some ways, and not so much in others. But I haven't forgotten our last conversation."

"It would be unwise if you did. But listen, I can't stay long, and I couldn't not show up. I just wanted to stop by and personally wish you a happy birthday."

Asha looked down as he removed a slender, gift-wrapped present from his inner coat pocket. "Rev', you didn't have to get me nothing."

He smiled. "If a person came to your party without bearing a gift, you'd be a fool to confuse them for a genuine friend. Happy birthday, little sister."

As she accepted the present, the Reverend instructed her not to open it yet. "Wait until later. It isn't much, so you might embarrass me if you open it now."

She saw the twinkle of humor in his eyes and grinned, "You think you're a slick old man, Rev'." After a parting embrace, Asha watched as he gracefully moved through the crowd before reaching the exit. She looked down at the gift, wondering how life would've been had her father been present. *You punk mu'fucka,* she inwardly cursed him.

Placing the gift in her pocket, Asha turned to see Teer and his team turning up. "Aye, Asha!" He threw up his hands, one of which held a gold champagne bottle. "Aye, yo, this party off the chain, my baby!"

Asha glanced at the off-duty officers posted throughout the club. "Teer, let this be your only bottle in here, okay? You're not even eighteen, love. But you can take some with you if you want."

"A'ight, I got you, my baby." He smiled, proudly displaying a white gold grille that sparkled with diamonds. "But I'm saying, I heard you got 42 Dugg and Dej Loaf coming through. Wassup with that?"

For a pretty penny, Asha had indeed booked the two artists to perform several songs later that night. "Yeah, they'll be here by ten."

Teer looked back at his team. "What I tell you niggas? And y'all thought I was perpin'."

Knowing she was responsible for Teer and his underage team being dipped in designer highlighted by diamonds, Asha couldn't help but observe them with a slight sense of pride. Although her field of employment was sinful by society's standards, she was just feeding her flock with the ingredients she had.

After reminding Teer to be mindful of his alcohol intake, Asha encouraged them to have fun before moving around. She next bumped into Bolo, her head security guard. "Wassup with the birthday girl? You need to dump a nigga on his head yet?"

Asha smiled. "Nah, not yet, but the night still young."

It was Bolo who hired the off-duty officers. After Asha mentioned the idea of having additional security for the night, he informed her of his friends who were members of SWAT. She had reluctantly given him the green light, and now wondered if her reluctance was the warning of a future mistake.

"Bolo, let me ask you something, between us."

"Of course," he replied, as if secrecy was a given.

"I know these your friends, and they're off-duty, but do you think they on some super-cop shit up in here?"

Bolo busted out in laughter, to which he put out a hand and quickly apologized. "My fault, Queen, I didn't mean no disrespect. But what you thinking so far from the truth that it's actually funny. But now can I say something to you, between us?" When she nodded, he lowered his tone and confided, "They make more on the side than they do at their job. So trust me, you ain't got nothing to worry about."

Relieved, Asha was about to ask what they did on the side, when she spotted a potential problem enter the party. "Excuse me, Bolo, let me get back with you."

Bearing a box-shaped gift with a bow on top, it was Angel who made the unwanted appearance. She smiled as Asha approached her. "Happy birthday, twin!"

Asha voiced her thanks and gave Angel a halfhearted hug.

"Listen, I didn't come here to start no trouble, or ruin your night," Angel explained. "But obviously I care about Noni, and I'll never forget about our little queen-pin move. So I just wanted to bring y'all a present and hopefully have fun."

Asha didn't doubt that Angel had a good heart. In fact, the girl was actually cool to kick it with. And her contribution to their cause would always be remembered. But when her brother felt like their friendship was a conflict of interest, Asha had no choice but to turn a cold shoulder.

For the advancement of an empire she'd set out to erect, there were only a select few people who Asha would allow to compromise her plans - and Angel wasn't one of them. But for the sake of her feelings, Asha would keep it cordial. And recalling what the Reverend had earlier said, the girl had indeed shown up with a gift.

"Alright, well, there's plenty of food and drinks," Asha welcomed her to the party. "But I'm telling you now, Angel, I don't want no fussing or fighting between you and my sister."

Angel held up her hand as a gesture of swearing under oath. "You got my word."

As Asha watched Angel head towards the bar, she realized there was still one important face she still hadn't seen - Noni's. Where the hell was her sister?

Coming from the back room, Lo-Lo and Shawna were giggling at something as Asha walked up. "Wassup, y'all seen Noni?"

They answered they hadn't, with Lo-Lo suggesting, "Maybe she forgot something at the hotel and went back to get it."

"But why wouldn't she say something?" Asha thought aloud. "Why wouldn't she tell me she was about to leave?"

"I'm not telling you not to worry," Shawna pitched in, "but knowing Noni, she probably up to something."

No sooner than she said that, the club's entrance door opened and someone walked in. Upon seeing who it was, the crowd went still, with their expressions reflecting shock and surprise. As if seeing a ghost, they couldn't believe the visual before their eyes.

Shawna covered her mouth in sheer disbelief. "Oh. My. God."

Standing before them was BFM Noni— who was shockingly dressed and made-up like a girl. Clad in an outfit identical to Asha's, her hair hung in loose curls, with her features made feminine by Covergirl products.

Asha thought her brain would explode from euphoric sensations. It had been years since her and her twin bore the same appearance. Growing emotional, she rushed to grip Noni in a fierce embrace. This was her baby and no one else's.

"Happy birthday, twin," Noni wished her big sister.

"Happy birthday, baby," Asha tearfully returned. "I love you so much. And I promise not to ever be mean to you again. You my little baby and you know it."

When they disengaged, Asha held Noni at arm's length and smiled. "You look so pretty."

Pleased by the compliment, Noni replied, "I just wanted to look like your twin for the day."

Feeling the lively effects of his champagne consumption, Teer interrupted their moment with a message for Noni. "Aye, yo, I ain't even gon' lie." He looked her up and down before bobbing his head. "You a bad mu'fucka."

As Noni and others joined in laughter, she playfully pushed him. "Nigga, if you don't get your lil' drunk, horny ass away from me!"

Noni felt the intensity of someone's stare and turned to lock eyes with Angel— who Noni couldn't deny was looking like a snack. But she maintained a Poker Face and simply lifted her head.

Angel closed the distance with a nervous expression. The present wasn't all she had brought to the party; as she also came with the hopes of giving Noni her second gift behind closed doors. She reached out for a hug. "Happy birthday, Noni."

Noni's nostrils were filled with a sweet-smelling fragrance as she held on to Angel. She told herself that it didn't make sense for a human being's scent to smell so damn good. Under different circumstances, Noni knew Angel would've been her special person.

"I brought you a present and I hope you like it," Angel continued. She then lowered her voice and added, "but I was hoping to give you your other present later tonight. I mean, that's if you don't already have plans."

There was a look so hopeful in Angel's eyes, that Noni didn't have the heart to outright crush her hopes. "Look, I'ma keep it a buck, my baby. I'm 'bout to get drunk as fuck and I don't know how the night gon' unfold. So, I don't wanna make no promise I might can't keep. And like I said, that's just me being real."

Visibly disappointed, Angel was on the verge of responding, when Lo-Lo intervened. "I'm sorry, Angel, but I need to borrow my girl for a second. I gotta get a picture of this!"

As the pair laughingly walked off, Angel scolded herself for the self-induced torture. *Why do you keep doing this to yourself? Why'd you even come here?*

When Angel took back her gift and stormed out the club, Shawna had observed her in quiet concern. Hurt people hurt people, which was something Shawna had learned from her own grandmother. And from the aching she'd seen in Angel's expression, Shawna knew it was something worth mentioning to Asha; for a scorned woman would swim to great lengths if it meant getting even.

A worrier by nature, Shawna returned to the back room for the umpteenth time. Punching in a four-digit code on the keypad, she opened the door and smiled in relief at the sight of Polaris on the floor, playing with her toys. She had to fight back tears, when the little girl looked up and unselfishly offered her one of the Barbies.

"No, baby, it's okay," Shawna softly declined, "I'm just checking up on you."

"She's such a sweet little girl," the hired nanny spoke up from her seat on the couch. "If I could only get my kids to be so well-behaved."

Without a family member or friend they could trust with Polaris, the girls had to hire an online nanny. Distrustful of leaving Polaris with a stranger, Shawna had firmly decided the back room would serve as the little girl's daycare. This was her way of attending the party, while keeping tabs on the tike at the same time.

After pressing her lips to Polaris' forehead, Shawna reminded the nanny to call her if the child so much as coughed. Touched by obvious affection Shawna had for the child, the woman assured her she'd do nothing less.

Upon her return to the party, Shawna looked around before sneaking over to the DJ's booth where she whispered a special request. Her heartbeat fluttered with excitement as she quickly walked off.

The four girls were gathered together, giggling at Noni being silly, when a John Legend song suddenly came on. The twins instantly locked eyes, as this was one of their favorite songs titled *Who Do We Think We Are*.

Wearing a mischievous grin, Shawna gave Asha a gentle nudge, to which Asha regarded her with a questioning look. Then it dawned on her, Shawna must've secretly watched how her and Noni listened to the song at home. "You little demon, you." Asha grinningly pinched Shawna on the arm.

"Go ahead," Shawna encouraged her in a near pleading tone. She just wanted the crowd to witness the beauty of the two sister's bond.

Asha looked at Noni who shrugged in response, then took her sister by the hand and led the way to the stage. When they mounted its steps, every head in the club curiously turned in their direction.

Lightly clapping in excitement as she knew what was coming, Shawna turned to Lo-Lo and beamed, "Watch this!"

Enfolding each other in a loving embrace, the twins began with a simple two-step. They then closed their eyes and continued to sway; allowing the moment and music to mesh with their spirits. Upon opening their eyes at the exact same time, they exchanged a smile before Asha raised Noni's arm and twirled her in a circle. It was then their movements grew magical, as they interlocked their left hands and did a matching routine that could've earned them a slot on Dancing With The Stars.

Every eye in the club watched the stage in amazement; with majority never knowing the two girls could dance to such a skillful degree.

Shawna wiped away tears as she focused on her friends with an expression of fondness. For her it was more than the graceful-like moves and fancy footwork. It was the language of love they spoke through their eyes. The way the twins stared at each other throughout the entire routine, it was as if nothing else mattered but their love for each other. Though Shawna couldn't relate to the coveted experience, she truly adored the connection the twin sisters shared.

Amid cheers and applause, the twins ended their act with a hug and a kiss on the cheek. When they looked out at the crowd full of marveled expressions, they looked back at each other, busted out in laughter and hugged again.

Making their way through the crowd, with people patting them on the back and complimenting their performance, the twins reunited with Lo-Lo and Shawna near the edge of the bar.

"You been crying?" Asha asked Shawna, as she noticed the redness of her eyes.

Shawna waved her hand. "Don't mind me, girl, these happy tears. Seeing y'all up there like that just..."

"Shawna, I'm warning you now." Noni pointed her finger and threatened, "if you start that shit up in here tonight, you going up on that stage next."

"But, Noni, you know I can't dance!" Shawna fearfully shrieked.

"Well, you better tighten up, then. Because if you embarrass me, with all that crying and shit, I'ma embarrass your ass right back. Now, what you wanna do?"

Shawna sniffed. "I'ma tighten up."

"A'ight, then. Now reach back there and grab me a bottle of Bubbly, so BFM Noni can find her something lovely!"

As they chuckled at Noni rhymes, Asha saw a lone Double-O posted up in the cut; with his hands wedged in his pants pockets. Her perceptive eyesight instantly noticed two things: the look of loss in his eyes, and CJ's absence.

"Wassup wit' it, bro?" Asha greeted Double-O as she joined him on the wall.

Without turning, he shook his head and answered, "I'm good. Just staying alert, you feel me?"

She nodded, then casually inquired, "Where CJ at? I know he know better than to miss my birthday."

There was a lapse of silence before Double-O replied, "Some niggas ain't cool with being Yayo; they wanna be Fifty." He looked at Asha and added with conviction, "But loyalty is law."

Double-O was referring to the rapper and business mogul 50 Cent, and his loyal partner, Tony Yayo. 50 was the boss, but Yayo was content with his assigned position; which was why he was still in picture increasing his figures. Unlike so many others who missed out on their blessings, Tony Yayo's humility led him to learn and accept his own limitations.

Familiar with the story of 50 Cent and Tony Yayo, Asha gained further insight into Double-O's character. Beside her was a warrior who saw the true value in virtue. And it was in that moment she determined he was worthy of being the recipient of something she'd given to no other man. Her trust.

Asha put an arm around Double-O, as if she was the big sister. "We might not be blood, but we definitely related through loyalty. You my brother, 'O, and for as long as I'm alive I'll never turn my back on you. And I put that on my wings, my creed, and my word as a woman."

Believing her disclosure with his whole entire heart, Double-O felt something he hadn't felt since the death of his best friend, King— completion. His love language was acts of service, so for him there was no greater source of fulfillment than being supportive of his friends.

Upon her phone buzzing from an incoming text message, Asha read it and told Double-O to come with her. "They're here."

They brought Dej Loaf and 42 Dugg in through the club's back entrance. Accompanied by a entourage of certified killers, the pint-size rappers were draped in designer and enough flawless diamonds to open up a Zales.

The crowd flew into a frenzy as the DJ announced their presence in the building. "So without further ado, y'all welcome to the stage, Dej Loaf and 42 Dugg!"

With androids and iPhone's recording the event, the crowd chanted the lyrics as the two Detroit natives performed their joint anthem, *Hard Times.*

"Where was you when it was hard times? A lot of these niggas mad that I made it/ acting like they happy, deep down know they hating..."

Paid to perform a total of three songs, 42 Dugg did a solo off his latest album, before Dej Loaf ended the night with her hit single, *Try Me.*

Ducked off in a corner of the club with Double-O, Asha wore a subtle grin of satisfaction as she took in the memorable event she had managed to create. While this day was designed to be mainly about her, she found more joy in making others happy.

As she and security escorted the rappers to the club's back entrance, Asha thanked them for showing up, to which they replied the pleasure was theirs. "And don't think we ain't hip to you, my baby." Dej Loaf smiled. "We know your lil' young ass out here putting on for the city."

"And it's Detroit versus everybody!" Dugg chimed in. "So, hit us anytime."

Asha watched the Sprinters disappear around the building and went back inside. Despite being appreciative of the rapper's appearance, Asha had made it clear to her crew in advance that they'd have to play the background. "...yeah, they famous, and they from the city, but we ain't 'bout to act like no groupies. We the Mob and we getting paper, too. So we gon' keep it cute, and keep it business. Straight like that." Because there was no denying her spiel made sense, neither girl had a problem with following her orders. And besides, it wasn't like they were aspiring rappers looking for a record deal.

It was near midnight and the party was officially over.

"What we gon' do about all this stuff?" Shawna quietly asked in reference to the tables full of gifts. Having relieved the nanny, she cradled a sleeping Polaris on her hip.

Asha looked around at the tables and the surrounding mess in which the club had been left. "What, y'all trying to clean this shit up tonight?"

"Hell nah!" Noni protested, clutching a bottle by the neck. "I don't know about none of y'all, but I got me another party lined up for the night."

Lo-Lo quickly averted her eyes, as she also had plans of her own.

"Alright, well, I guess it'll give us something to do tomorrow," Asha concluded.

Trailed by Bolo and his security team, the group filed outside to the parking lot, where Noni started looking around as she realized something. "Aye, Double-O, where CJ at? I just realized I ain't heard that nigga mouth none tonight."

Double-O confessed in code, "Dog got sick, so I had to give him some medicine to help him sleep."

In the split second it took for Noni to catch on, she first frowned in confusion, then her eyebrows rose at the sudden realization. Despite her desire to hear all the details, she played it cool and casually replied, "Yeah, well, that nigga missed a hell-of-a party. But we definitely don't need him spreading them germs."

The night was still young, and Asha decided it would be unfair to interfere with their fun. Noni had a date, Lo-Lo clearly had Uno on the brain, and the way Double-O stood close to Shawna as she held that baby- they reflected the image of a close-knit family.

"Aye, y'all, I need to talk to Bolo about something," Asha lied, "so y'all go ahead and leave without me."

Noni shrugged at the senselessness of her suggestion. "A'ight, we'll just wait for you, then."

Asha shook her head, to which Noni asked, "Then how you gon' get home?"

"I don't know. I can get a Uber or something," Asha impatiently answered. "Now, will y'all go so I can talk to this man?"

Lo-Lo narrowed her eyes in suspicion. "You met somebody, didn't you?"

Asha fed into her false assumption by smiling. "No, I didn't meet nobody."

"Noni, you hear this?" Lo-Lo exclaimed. "She think she slick. She done met somebody!"

But Noni didn't bite. She knew her sister too well, and didn't believe she had a man on her mind. But whatever it was, she had her reasons. So Noni gave her a hug and a kiss and told her to be careful.

As Asha watched them drive out the lot, she swallowed the lump in her throat and fought back tears. This was the birthday she awaited ever since she could remember... and who would've thought her final gift of the night would be a feeling of loneliness.

Chapter 17

"Uno, please!" Lo-Lo cried, as he had her folded in half on the living room floor of his apartment. "You hurting my stomach, daddy!"

His bronze-colored skin glistening with sweat, he ignored her cries and continued to crush her at a merciless rate. "Tell me you sorry!" He barked in between his barbaric assault.

"Oh my god, daddy!" She clawed at the carpet and the skin of his back.

"Bitch, I said tell me you sorry," he forced himself deeper in the dampness of her tunnel. "Tell me you sorry for cuffing this pussy."

With her eyes rolled upwards as she wore a pained grimace, she obediently yelled, "I'm sorry!"

"Sorry for what?" He demanded, digging even deeper. She screamed in response, to which he repeated, "Sorry for what?"

Hardly able to breathe, she managed to moan, "For cuffing this pussy."

"Now tell me you won't do it again!"

As she felt him break through her will and take captive of her soul, she gave in to the invasion and surrendered all control. "I won't do it again."

He slowed his stroke, taking pride in the tears that escaped from the corners of her eyes. But with his quest incomplete, he brought her with him as he stood up from the floor; careful to keep himself buried in her tunnel. Then, gripping her butt cheeks, he held her in midair and resumed his rough treatment.

Squeezing her arms around his neck, she screamed in his chest as he repeatedly slammed her on his stone-like erection. She was certain that when she left this apartment it would be to the nearest mental asylum— for this maniac clearly meant to drive her insane.

After ensuring every tenant in the building knew his name, he carried her into his room and threw her on the bed. "Now turn your ass over, so I can smoke it from the back!"

Once she was on all fours with her face in the pillow, he spread both cheeks, pressed his lips to her yoni, his nose to her butthole, then literally attempted to suck out her uterus.

She screamed, which caused him to seemingly suck even harder. She tried to run, but he snatched her back and locked her place. Then, when she pushed on his head to try and fight him off, he captured her clit with his lips and caused her whole body to suddenly lock up; forcing her to succumb to the torture of his tongue.

She came in his mouth and he drank every drop. "That's how you smoke it from the back." He smiled, licking his lips of her flavorful frosting. But he still had unfinished business.

"Daddy, I need a break," she uselessly pled as he rolled her over. "You gon' kill me."

As he proceeded to please her at a love-making pace, he leaned down to kiss her tear-stained face before speaking four words she never thought she would hear, "I love you, Lo-Lo."

Returning his stare with a starry-eyed expression, she shed a fresh set of tears and so tenderly replied, "I love you, too, daddy."

The twins had each other. Shawna had Polaris. And now Lo-Lo was certain she had her special person. After longing for love since her adolescent years, she believed in heart Uno was her future husband.

But if only she knew what the future had in store.

**

Inside a hotel room on the city's outskirts, Noni went to work on the woman in front of her. "This that Noni dick!" She boasted while taking occasional sips from a Belaire bottle. With her hair pulled back into a braided ponytail, she wore a Nike sports bra and a foot-long strap that veered to the left. And if you assumed she was slipping, she was facing the front door with a full-size Glock within reach.

Noni paused her performance to pour a drop of champagne over the shaft of her strap. Flashing her teeth at the recording camera of her phone, she took a generous sip and pressed play on her performance.

Though Noni was enjoying herself, this encounter had little to do with pleasure, but was more out of spite. Because in Noni's opinion, there was nothing like deflating a haughty man's ego.

Tossing the empty bottle aside, Noni grabbed the woman by the waist and made her wail louder than three newborns. "That nigga can't fuck you like this, can he?"

The woman screamed he couldn't into the cotton of the sheets. While she'd been with a number of men and a fair share of women, BFM Noni was in a league of her own. This light skin, tatted-up, diamond-tooth stud served the best pound-cake on a platinum-covered platter.

Ready to change positions, Noni slowly withdrew from the recess of her womb. She smirked at the syrup-like evidence of her pleasurable skills. "Aye, yo, let me borrow your mouth right quick," she slapped the woman on her bottom. "I need to mop up this mess you done made back here."

When she turned and brought her face into view, it was none other than the woman who'd been with the man who Noni fought in the parking lot. She went viral for fighting him, and now she'd go viral for sexing the woman he wanted for a wife.

As the woman used her lips and tongue to cleanse the strap, Noni looked at the camera and smirked. "When you niggas gon' learn you can't turn a hoe into a housewife?"

Chapter 18

With Polaris asleep in the backseat, Double-O and Shawna were parked by a deserted waterfront. In spite of Shawna being a lifelong resident of Detroit, she had never known this location existed. It was abandoned but beautiful, rendering a soothing sense of serenity.

As she gazed out at the water, she disturbed the silence with a quiet inquiry. "How do you know about this place?"

"Puma," he answered, instantly gaining him Shawna's attention. "She used to come here a lot. She said it helped her think. And since I've been out, I come here sometimes."

Shawna observed him. "You really loved her, didn't you?"

He slowly nodded. "She was like my big sister." Double-O lowered his head and regretfully admitted, "But I let her down in the end."

Shawna had lived with Puma up until her death, so she already knew the cause of his guilt. Basically, Double-O and his best friend, King, had decided they'd be better off climbing the rungs of riches alone. But their move was inspired by Mecca's plan to divide and conquer; which in the end is exactly what happened. She divided their tribe, then conquered them all, one-by-one. Stuck with the bitter aftermath of her malicious actions, Double-O blamed himself for the toppling of his team and carried in his heart a survivor's remorse.

"I understand how you feel, but Puma wasn't mad at you," Shawna truthfully revealed. He looked at her as if weighing her honesty, and Shawna continued, "She had talked to me about it, right before she passed. And she understood that you was just being loyal to King, and that King was being misled by that woman, Unique. So if anything, Puma was more frustrated than angry. Because she couldn't figure out how to fix her family. But you gotta get rid of that guilt, because I promise you, Puma loved you just as much as you loved her."

Double-O found immeasurable comfort in what he believed to be an honest revelation. And up until the current conversation, he thought Puma hated him in the final moments of her untimely demise. So for Shawna to tell him otherwise, it lessened the weight of a burden he'd been carrying for years.

"But she might be mad at *me*, though," Shawna added with a nervous chuckle.

"Why you say that?"

"You remember her gun? The one she named Martha?"

Double-O nodded, vividly recalling the Glock that bore nicks of her total number of kills.

"Well, I ended up with it on the day she went missing, and I kept it for all these years. So anyways, I showed it to the twins one day, and I saw how Noni looked at it. And since she reminds me of Puma so much, I decided to give it to her for her birthday."

When Shawna had presented Noni with the pistol, she'd never forget the reflection of reverence on Noni's face. How she had held it with the delicacy of a brand-new baby; vowing to regularly clean it, and to add to its body-count in memory of Puma.

It was Double-O's turn to cover up Shawna with a blanket of comfort. "Nah, I think you did the right thing by giving it to her. Because if there was anybody Puma would want to have it, ain't no doubt in my mind it would be Noni. Because not only is she active, but her heart don't got a dark spot in it. And the way she be putting in work..." He cracked a slight grin at her history of violence. "She definitely gon' make Puma proud."

After a lapse of silence, Shawna hesitantly spoke, "Aye, um, I ain't trying to be all nosey or nothing, but I'm curious about something."

Label it luck or intuition, but Double-O read her mind and replied, "I killed him. But I had to. Because his character got sick, and murder was the only medicine I could give him."

"Oh damn," was Shawna's startled response upon hearing his candid confession. He had caught her off guard with that one. But then she thought about something and turned back to question, "Aye, how did you know what I wanted to ask?"

"I just felt it." He shrugged.

As their extended stare exchanged blended emotions, the sudden acceleration of Shawna's heartbeat caused her to quickly turn away. *Oh my god! Oh my god!* She inwardly panicked, thinking her eardrums would burst from the pounding of her heart.

"Shawna, I didn't mean to make you uncomfortable," Double-O apologized. "So that's my fault if I did."

"Double-O, it ain't you, it's me. I've been through a whole lot in a little bit of time. I got issues I don't know if I'll ever be able to fix. So right now, I couldn't offer more than a friendship to you, or anybody else for that matter. I hope you can understand."

"Probably more than you know," he replied, recalling a damaging childhood that left him with physical scars and a distrust of women.

Double-O and Shawna were two tortured souls who had unknowingly been raised by the same pair of parents. Pain and Suffering.

***

After sending her crew on their way, Asha told Bolo he'd been used as an excuse, wished him a good night and took off walking. He had called out her name in concern for her safety, to which she threw up peace sign and kept it moving. Whether you were on wheels or feet, Asha's belief was that fate was a force you couldn't avoid. So what was the point of being imprisoned by fear. And besides, she could stand the exercise.

Along her leisure stroll through downtown, where she seemed to notice certain establishments for the first time, Asha's thoughts were all over the place. Like, how she had her sisters, yet sometimes still felt lonely. Like, how she had a full bank account, yet still felt a hollowness on her insides. Like, how she, too, wanted to experience love, yet couldn't find a cure for her phobia of men. And like, how she was actually curious about her father, yet was simply too stubborn to grant him forgiveness. To the world Asha Kincaid might've appeared to have it together, but she was really just an ordinary girl with more problems than solutions.

Unaware of the Mercedes Benz truck that drove past, Asha reached the MGM and strode through its parking lot. *The glass always half full*, she told herself, deciding she would enjoy the remainder of her night, even if it was spent alone.

Inside the suite, Asha stripped naked, grabbed her a chilled bottle of champagne and headed for her famous sanctuary— the bathroom.

Pretty hurts/ we shine the light on whatever's worse/ you're trying to fix something, but you can't fix what you can't see/ it's the soul that needs surgery.

Asha was submerged in bubbles as she listened to one of her favorite Beyoncé songs on repeat— *Pretty Hurts*. She had her eyes closed, held a glass of champagne in one hand and a lit joint in the other.

While Asha didn't normally indulge in the plant-based drug, tonight marked a special occasion. And with the suite all to herself, she also decided she would close out the night with one of her close friends.

Asha took a small toke, a generous sip, and continued to groove with her girl, Queen Bey - the stranger who seemed to sing to her soul.

On the table next to the tub was Asha's phone and a piece of paper with a number written on it. The number belonged to the boy, Jaylen, who attended her college. She had actually considered calling him. In fact, she had had the phone in her hand and was dialing the number, when she got cold feet and ditched the idea.

When on her third glass of bubbly and nearly halfway through the joint, Asha experienced a floating sensation. "Ooh, I'm tipsy." She giggled, leaning over to stub out the joint and set the glass down. She then reached beneath the water and pulled the plug.

Once the water had drained out the tub, she lowered the music and called out, "Aye, girl, where you at? I'm ready!"

After a few seconds passed without receiving a response, Asha peered over the edge of the tub, then smiled, "Oh, there you are."

Posing on the table, sporting her traditional pink outfit, was Asha's bff, "Big Rose". No matter the place or the time of day, Big Rose always rose to the occasion. She was such a faithful friend, which was why Asha faithfully kept her fully charged.

With the device in hand and her clitoris throbbing in wild anticipation, Asha turned Beyoncé back up, buried Big Rose between her thighs and blissfully rode on her rollercoaster ride!

Chapter 19

On a west side street called Dexter, a group of the grimiest looking men in the Motor were gathered outside, when a '69 Camaro SS came flying up the block. Candy-purple with matching shoes, the coupe squealed to a stop before the driver cut the wheel and reversed into the driveway of the house at which the men were gathered.

Unfolding himself from the car was Uno, who sported a plain pair of Carti's and a Polo tracksuit. As he greeted each Band Gang member with a solid embrace, he spotted his cousin, D-Nutty, on the porch, and had a pretty good idea why his presence had been summoned.

"Wassup wit' my nigga Uno?" His friend, Guru, smiled as they embraced. "What's good, my baby?"

"I'm chilling, brodie." Uno returned the smile. "Just trying to pen something platinum, you feel me?"

Rocking shoulder-length dreads with red tips, Guru bobbed his head in agreement. "Yeah, I feel that. Because niggas definitely trying to transition from trapping and jacking to full-time rapping. And I'm saying..." Guru grinned. "From what I'm hearing, nigga, you got the cheat code. So take me with you, my baby."

"And how I'm supposed to do that?"

Guru looked away and scoffed as if he couldn't believe his intelligence had just been insulted. At 5'9" and a chiseled one-eighty-five, Guru was as dangerous as they came; which was why D-Nutty had put a bug in his ear.

Not one for the games, Guru waved for D-Nutty's presence. When D-Nutty walked up, Guru asked, "Did you or did you not tell me this nigga fucking on one of them Butterfly Mafia hoes?"

"I did," D-Nutty affirmed. "He fucking the white one." After CJ's unfortunate and untimely death, D-Nutty decided it was time to force Uno's hand by involving the clan.

Guru looked at Uno and clasped his hands behind his back. "So, you don't know what he talking about?"

"I'm saying, this weird ass nigga want me to bite my own bitch in the back. And this ain't that. I'm rocking with the hoe, Blood."

"So, basically, you saying you willing to put a white bitch before the gang. That's what you telling me, right?"

Uno drew a deep breath to compose himself. He cut his eyes at his cousin, thinking to himself, *I should've been killed this nigga.* But Uno had a plan. One that he prayed would pacify his piranha-like peoples. "Guru, you ain't never known me to do no fuck-shit in all the time you've known me," Uno began. "So, I can't believe you questioning my character right now, let alone my loyalty. But to prove that I keep my peoples in mind, I think I gotta way we all can eat."

D-Nutty frowned, for he was certain that whatever Uno had in mind was contrary to what he had on his.

"Instead of trying to rob 'em for whatever we can get," Uno continued, "I can get 'em to front us some bricks, and we can eat way more like that. Why settle for scraps, when we can get a seat at the table and eat off plates, you feel me? Come on, my baby, we too player to be scavengers."

As Guru considered the proposal, D-Nutty quickly poured poison all over it. "Now this nigga trying to turn these bitches into our bosses. He trying to have us working for the hoes. Talking 'bout 'fronting us some bricks'. Nigga, if you don't get your tender-dick-ass outta here."

To everyone's surprise, Uno snatched D-Nutty up by his collar. "Ain't nothing tender about me, Blood!"

135

When Guru and several others pried the two cousins apart, D-Nutty was holding a chrome handgun. "Nigga, I should give you a leg-warmer," he growled at Uno, referring to a gunshot in the leg.

"Put that up, gang, you fooling," Guru instructed D-Nutty. "This your relative, nigga." D-Nutty didn't immediately comply and Guru stepped closer. "Blood, you ain't hear what the fuck I just said? Put that mu'fucka up before you turn this into something different."

"I'm just saying..." D-Nutty huffed, reluctantly replacing the weapon to his waistline. "This nigga put his hands on me. And I don't—"

"Well, put your hands on him back!" Guru cut him off. "What, you scared to square-up with this nigga, or something? You need a nigga to teach you how to box, Blood? Is that what it is?"

Amid chuckles in the crowd, D-Nutty had steam coming from his flared nostrils. If Guru wasn't the capo of their clan, D-Nutty would publicly stain the pavement with particles of his brain.

"But back to you," Guru said, returning his attention to Uno. "I don't think I'm feeling the idea of working for no hoes, either. I'ma have to roll with D-Nutty on this one. Fuck them bitches, and fuck they bricks. If you wanna wife-up a white hoe, that's on you, gang. But I'ma need you to get to bottom of it. It could be a robbery, or it can be a massacre. But either way, we need parts. Big parts. So figure it out, my baby. And we'll use what we take to build our own bridge."

Uno eyed Guru as if he couldn't be serious. "So you willing to go to war and risk lives and freedom, over some shit I can get for *free?*"

"Nigga, we talking about a group of hoes," a man near Guru commented. "I'll wipe them bitches down my-muthafucking-self."

"Nigga, you ain't never kilt *shit*," Uno shot back. "And you talking like Noni and that nigga, Double-O, don't own a graveyard. So shut yo' dumb ass up."

Uno looked back at Guru and reasoned, "Ain't no war ever been won without there being casualties on both sides. So, all I'm saying is, let's pick our battles wisely, you feel me? I can get more for free, than what we can take by force. So make it make sense, my baby."

Having been to federal prison in the past, Guru jokingly adopted the dialect of a DC native, "You a wild nigga, slim." He smiled at Uno. "For real, moe. You out here *lunching* and shit. You hear me?"

Guru turned to lift his head at a man who stood by the curb. "Wassup, gang, you scared to go to war, my nigga?"

In a wordless response, the man removed the lid of a trashcan, reached in and withdrew a 100-round Draco.

"What about you, Blood?" Guru lifted his head at a second man, who jogged to a trashcan across the street and removed an AK-47.

With both men brandishing fully operable assault rifles, Guru draped an arm around Uno and smirked. "As you can see, we ain't worried about no war, my baby. And especially not when one of our own in the bed with the other side. So you just stick to figuring it out..." He patted Uno's chest in encouragement, "and let me handle this gangsta shit."

After watching Uno hop back in his car and speed off down the block, Guru turned to look at D-Nutty and busted out laughing. "I still can't believe you let dog snatch you up like that! That nigga had you up off your feet. Your shit was dangling, Blood."

As the crowd of men roared in laughter with Guru, he added, "Man, somebody go get me some boxing gloves, so I can take son-son in the backyard and teach him how to fight."

Regretting his decision to seek Guru's help, D-Nutty didn't know who wanted to shoot first... Guru or his cousin.

But he was certain of one thing - Uno was his family through blood, but no longer through loyalty.

***

"How long we gon' stay cooped up in this hotel?" Lo-Lo whined to Asha as they sat in the living room. "This like being on house arrest."

Asha looked at Shawna and nudged her head, to which Shawna took Polaris by the hand and led her out the room. "Come on, Sugar Bear, let's go play."

Once they were gone, Asha replied to Lo-Lo, "I'ma stay cooped up till I know exactly what's going on. I don't know if you forgot, but they hung that girl and made it look like suicide. That's some vicious shit, so I ain't putting nothing past whoever did it. And understand something, Lo'. I love you to death, but I'm not forcing you to stay. If you feel that man is more important than you safety... then be my guest."

"Man, I'm tired of biting my tongue," Noni interrupted before Lo-Lo could respond. "I'm saying, how the fuck and why the fuck is you still dealing with this nigga, and you don't even know if he tied in with this shit? Like, what if he is, then what?"

"But he's not," Lo-Lo stressed. "I'm telling y'all, Uno ain't like that. I ain't saying he ain't never did no dirt, I'm just saying that he wouldn't do nothing to bring harm to me or my loved ones. And he know y'all my loved ones."

Noni took a deep breath and clenched her fists in frustration. "Do you honestly hear how the fuck you sound right now? You vouching for a nigga you ain't even known for a whole year."

"But it don't take a year to—"

"Asha, get her!" Noni rose from the couch to put distance between herself and Lo-Lo. "She on that naïve-ass white girl shit!"

"Noni, I sent the baby in the other room for a reason," Asha patiently explained, "so please lower your voice, love."

As a result of Shawna's constant care and affection, Polaris now rarely had nightmares, had regained a normal appetite, and was even returning to her talkative self. So the last thing they needed was for her to be frightened back into a reclusive shell.

"I just don't understand why y'all being so hard on him," Lo-Lo said, growing emotional. "I mean, besides meeting him that one time, you don't even know him. And you can't base who he is off the company he keeps. That would be like saying that just because Shawna is tight with Noni, then that makes her a killer, too."

Lo-Lo knew what she said was a mistake as soon as it left her lips. But the damage was done, for there was no way to retract a spoken statement.

Though Asha understood that Lo-Lo's statement had been made out of her weakness for a man - and nothing more, Noni was offended on a personal level. "So that's what you see me as?" Noni walked down on Lo-Lo. "Not your sister, but a killer?"

"Noni, I'm sorry, I didn't mean it like."

"Well, that's how I took it. And if that's how you see me, it's what *you* turned me into. Don't forget how I got started."

"Noni," Asha called, shaking her head for her sister to stop.

"Nah, yo, she shouldn't have said no shit like that. Not when I caught my first body over *her*. When that nigga, Kenny-Boy, whooped off in your ass and you came running to us. All beat the fuck up and bloody and shit. I did that for you because you was my sister." Noni looked Lo-Lo up and down and scoffed. "Or so I thought."

Lo-Lo was now in tears. Why couldn't there be a bridge between love and loyalty? Why should she have to turn her back on a man who made her feel complete? And why couldn't they understand and accept that she had never been so happy?

This girl is in love, Asha thought, knowing it was pointless to interfere any longer. But Asha couldn't help but take partial blame, for she could've convinced Lo-Lo to cut Uno off long before that seed of lust had a chance to blossom into full-grown love.

Asha took Lo-Lo's hand. "You're making a serious mistake, love. And I would never purposely keep you from being with someone who made you happy. But you fell for the wrong man again, Lo'. And that's not to say his heart isn't right. So it might not be his teeth that bite you, but I promise you gon' get bit. Because can you honestly look me in my eyes and tell me he gotta leash on every dog in his pack?"

When Lo-Lo didn't answer or even look up, Asha concluded, "I just hope in the end, you can say it was worth it."

It took considerable courage, but Lo-Lo rose to her feet and went to go pack. When she returned minutes later, with her luggage in tow, she paused at the door and looked back at the twins. "Please, don't hate me for following my heart."

As the door clicked shut behind Lo-Lo's departure, neither girl could've predicted how their lives were about to dramatically unfold.

Chapter 20

"What we gon' do about, Lo-Lo?" Shawna asked Asha, as the two of them rode through the downtown area. "I'm worried about her, Asha."

"I'll tell you what we not gon' do," Asha said without taking her eyes off the road. "And that's worry about something we can't control. She made her decision, and it's out of our hands now."

"Yeah, but, y'all never gave up on me. And I did way worse than fall in love with some boy. So she just need our help, the same way y'all helped me. And regardless of her decision, she still our sister. So I don't think it would be right to just turn our back on her. I mean, don't you think that would be kind of hypocritical, being that—"

"Alright, alright, Shawna!" Asha threw her hand in surrender. "Damn, you win okay? Because clearly you ain't finna let this go. And since you clearly been thinking about it, why don't you tell me what Shawna suggests we do."

She studied her lap before quietly answering, "I was thinking we could..." She shrugged her shoulders. "You know."

"No, I don't know." Asha glanced at her. "You gotta give me more to work with than that."

"I was thinking that maybe we could, um, maybe have Noni... you know."

"Have Noni what?"

"You know, just maybe make Uno go away, that's all."

"What, you mean like, make him move out of town?" Asha replied, playing dumb to what she knew Shawna was suggesting.

"No, Asha, I mean like, make him go away forever."

"Ooh Shawna!" Asha feigned shock at her suggestion. "I can't believe you, girl. You ready to get this nigga whacked. You on your Mob shit for real."

"I'm just saying, I ain't a killer but don't push me," Shawna smilingly recited the lyrics of Tupac.

After they shared a laugh, Shawna added, "But for real, Asha. I don't think we'd be wrong for taking his life to save Lo-Lo's. Y'all had to literally put me in rehab to save me, and I just think that removing him from the picture will save her."

Asha's response was postponed as she turned into the parking lot of a large building. Still in the downtown vicinity, Asha had spotted the building during her walk last week.

"What's this?" Shawna inquired, as she took in a building that required major renovation.

"Your future," Asha said, exiting the truck. "Now come on, let's go check it out."

Upon entering the building, they wrinkled their noses at the lingering stench of mildew and mold. But aside from the smell, Asha thought the property was perfect.

"Look at all this space," Asha pointed out, as they took a tour of what was once a grocery store. "And don't you just like how everything is on one floor?"

"Asha, you still haven't told me how this is my future."

Asha stopped walking and took Shawna's hands. "You have a special way with children, love. And I'm not just talking about how much you've helped Polaris in such a short amount of time, but I'm speaking on children in general. They literally light up around you, girl. And they have that same effect on you. So I got to thinking, and I thought, 'why not open up Shawna a daycare? It'll be something she'll enjoy, and most importantly, it'll keep her out of harm's way."

"Wait, wait, wait," Shawna said, as she could feel herself becoming increasingly excited. "Are you telling me that this building, right here, the one we standing in right now, is gon' be my daycare?"

Asha beamed while nodding her head, "That's exactly what I'm telling you."

Shawna screamed. Then she started stomping her feet on the floor in euphoria. She gave Asha a kiss on each cheek, her forehead, then put her in a bear hug and picked her up. "Oh my God, I love you so much, girl!"

When Shawna finally let her go, she was struck with a sudden thought. "Ooh, what we gon' name it?"

"I was gon' leave that up to you."

Shawna pondered for a second, then looked at Asha with one of her worried expressions that always managed to tug at Asha's heart. "Asha, you know I'm not that creative. I'll be thinking forever before I come up with something. So, help me, girl, or this thing will never get opened."

Having already given it some thought, Asha said, "Well, I don't think it should be nothing too fancy. This gon' be a daycare, not a boutique. So, I was thinking we could go with what best describes you, being as though you'll be the owner."

Shawna rolled her hand in impatience. "Alright, so what you got? Spit it out."

Asha smiled. "We'll call it, Big Baby's. Because I'll be damned if you ain't no big ass baby!"

She kept repeating the name to herself before bobbing her head in approval. "Big Baby's. Yeah, I like that. And it sounds fun."

"Right," Asha confirmed. "And it's inviting. Like, who wouldn't want to drop their kids off at Big Baby's? And then once they walk in and see your lil' chocolate face... aw man, it's a wrap. They gon' be bringing you kids from all over Michigan."

Shawna envisioned a room full of children, laughing and playing. This would be more than a daycare, it would be a home away from home. And if she saw a parent struggling, she'd approach them in private and offer to help out. And she'd keep track of every child's birthday, ensuring that each received a party and presents.

Smiling at the prospect, Shawna couldn't wait until the business was open. "So when we gon' start fixing this place up? Because it clearly needs a lot of work. And I'm ready to get started."

"Now you know we not about to get our pretty little hands dirty. I already hired a crew to take care of it. Matter fact, it's the same crew that did the club. We just gon' sit back and bark orders."

Shawna eyed Asha with a look of amazement. "You only twenty-one, love. And sometimes I wonder if you've actually sat back and acknowledged everything you've accomplished. Whether it was legal or not, you still put your mind to it and made it happen. Girl, we own one of the most popular clubs in the city. We literally live on the top floor of the MGM. And now we about to own a daycare. But none of this would be possible if it wasn't for you. I love you so much, Asha. And I know there's no way I can match everything you've done for me. But I promise to be your best friend forever, and to do everything in my power to make you proud of me."

The two girls hugged again, with Asha telling Shawna she loved her more, and that she was already proud of her. "But you know what would make me even prouder?" Asha said as they disengaged, "for you to put all your focus into this daycare business."

"What do you mean?"

"Listen, you'll always be Butterfly Mafia, but I want you to separate yourself to a certain extent."

"But, Asha, I don't—"

"Just hear me out," Asha cut in. "Because, Shawna, you gotta think, you got that little girl to look after now. And what happens to her if something happens to you? And if I keep allowing you to be in the middle of everything, then I can't guarantee that something won't happen. So until I figure out how to fully transition, and not be mixed in with anything that'll jeopardize our lives and freedom, then I need you to fall back, love. The daycare and Polaris will keep you busy. You'll never need for money, so you could babysit kids for free if you wanted to. But at the end of the day, the main thing is, I'll know you're safe."

Shaking her in doubt, Shawna replied, "Asha, I don't know. I *love* being around you, girl. I love watching you and listening to you. I feel like being around you makes me stronger. And you don't know how much I've learned from you."

"You've learned enough!" Asha grabbed Shawna by her arms. "You gotta stop acting so helpless, girl. It's like you're your own worst critic. You don't give yourself credit for nothing. I know you've been belittled and mistreated in the past, but that don't take away from who you are as a person. What was done to you was because of *them*, not you. So if you really wanna make me proud, then you'll start believing in yourself and step up to that plate and swing."

Shawna had her head down.

"Look at me," Asha said, to which Shawna slowly lifted her head and Asha continued, "Whether you know it or not, you're just as strong as me, just in your own way. Yeah, I might make certain shit happen, but you've endured way more than me, and you're still standing - literally raising a child. Shawna... you gotta understand that all the help I've given you is what the universe wanted. And if it wasn't me, it would've picked someone else to give you the push you needed. Because this is all by design, love. You were destined to make it. If not, you'd be stuck in a way worse predicament right now, or maybe even dead. So, I'ma need you to cut out all that self-doubt, and start embracing what life is offering you."

They resumed their tour of the building, trading opinions on what should go where. "And I'm thinking I'll buy racecar beds for the boys, and something real pretty for the girls," Shawna explained, having regained her excitement. "And there'll be plenty of toys and video games. But I'll make sure that most of the games are educational. You know, so they can have fun and learn at the same time."

"Do whatever you want, love," Asha encouraged her, "because I already know you gon' have the best daycare in Detroit."

As Shawna continued sharing ideas, Asha got a text from Noni, which she read and interrupted Shawna, "I hate to cut you off, but I forgot that Noni got boxing practice. So we gotta go get her and Polaris and drop her off."

As they locked up the building, discussing Noni's upcoming fight, Shawna remembered something she'd been meaning to mention. "Aye, not to change the subject, but you remember when Angel came to the birthday party?" Asha said she did, to which Shawna continued, "Well, I don't know what happened, but she got real upset about something and took back her gift and stormed out the club. That woman angry, Asha. And in a way, I understand. I mean, she helped y'all with that one stuff y'all did, and introduced you to her brother. So I can see how she could be feeling like she got used."

They climbed in the truck and Asha replied, "Well, for one, I ended up giving her a fair share of that money. And two, it was her own brother who didn't approve of her hanging with us. If it hadn't been for that, Noni could've married her, for all I care. It wasn't like she wasn't cool to be around. But I was not about to slow down or jeopardize the progress of what we got going. My job is to make sure my loved ones are in winning positions, and everything outside of that is irrelevant."

"I hear you, Asha. But I'm just saying, that woman had a real hurt look on her face. And you always say not to underestimate nobody. So, I just hope she wouldn't do nothing to try to get back at you or Noni."

Shawna definitely made sense, which was an additional reason Asha couldn't wait to disassociate herself with anything street-related. No matter how much money they profited monthly, the risks were simply not worth the rewards.

No sooner than they turned out the building's parking lot, the gas light cut on. "Shit," Asha cursed, "Noni, ain't put no damn gas in this thing last night. I done told that girl about that. And you've heard me, Shawna."

"You know Noni be absentminded as hell." Shawna laughed. "And it ain't no telling what she was out doing last night."

Entering the nearest gas station, Asha pulled up to a pump and told Shawna she'd be right back, to which Shawna offered to get out and pump. "Nah, I just need you to keep coming up with ideas for that daycare," Asha replied, "and leave the gas pumping up to me. But do you want anything out of here?"

"Yeah, grab me some starburst and a juice. And get Polaris one of those suckers she likes."

As Shawna watched Asha go inside the gas station, she smiled to herself, thinking how grateful she was to have a friend so generous. "And she gon' say I'ma big ass baby." Shawna chuckled as she cut on some music.

Inside the gas station, Asha was waiting in line, when someone behind her requested her attention. "Excuse me."

Asha turned to stare into a pair of the prettiest green eyes. "Yes?"

"I'm sorry to bother you." Mecca smiled. "But I just had to compliment your hair. Girl, you rocking that shit."

With the assistance of clip-in extensions and clear elastics, Asha's latest hairstyle was a Bubble Pony, accented by layers of shiny bracelets. The Pony hung midway down her back, giving off the vibes of a womanly warrior.

"Thank you." Asha returned her smile. "And if only I had your eye color to match."

"Girl, I wish I could give 'em to you." Mecca laughed. "Let you see how it feels to hear so many corny-ass compliments from these niggas."

Forgetful of the sucker, Asha paid for her items in hand a full tank of gas.

"It was nice meeting you." Mecca waved as Asha turned to leave.

"Likewise," Asha replied, having no idea she had just traded pleasantries with the woman determined on seeing her dead.

Shawna lowered her window as Asha returned to the truck. "Where the sucker?" She asked, accepting the Starburst and two bottled drinks.

"Aw, damn, I forgot. This woman in there started talking to me, and it threw me off."

"Don't worry about it," Shawna said, reaching for the door handle. "Just pump the gas and I'll go in and grab it real quick."

Shawna was entering the gas station, when Mecca walked right past her; intensely focused on something ahead. Frozen in her tracks, Shawna couldn't believe they had again crossed paths, this time in Detroit. *Something ain't right*, she thought to herself before turning to leave. *I gotta warn Asha.*

As Shawna came around the front of the truck, she saw two things at nearly the same time— Asha pumping gas, and a masked figure creeping towards them in a crouched position. Shawna wanted to scream but her voice wouldn't work, as she was literally paralyzed in fear.

When Asha looked up and saw the horrified expression on Shawna's face, she didn't have to look back to know someone was behind her. Instead, she ran to Shawna and protectively placed her arms around her.

As the first two shots struck Asha in her back, she recalled the nightmare she'd had about Noni and now knew the dream really pertained to her. She was brought back to reality by the third gunshot, which tore into her shoulder.

Pinned between Asha and the truck, Shawna felt the impact of Asha absorbing all three gunshots. She was so afraid, thinking she'd never see Polaris again, or the opening day of Big Baby's daycare. But at least she would die in her best friend's arms.

The next shot hit Asha in the neck, causing her to hold on to Shawna even tighter. She knew her time was up, but she would use what little she had left to protect her girl. *I love you, Noni*, she thought in farewell, knowing fate was a force you couldn't avoid. *I love you so much, little baby.*

Asha's thoughts were shut off when the fifth and final shot hit her in back of the head. Because her arms were still wrapped around Shawna, Asha brought her along as she lifelessly collapsed to the ground.

At the sound of tires squealing in retreat, Shawna opened her eyes and her whole world was black. She initially thought she was dead, then realized the darkness came from being buried under Asha.

"Asha, I think they gone," Shawna quietly informed her. When Asha didn't respond, Shawna gently shook her. "Asha?"

As tears began coming out the corners of her eyes, Shawna carefully maneuvered Asha onto her back. Her heart shattered into a million pieces at the sight of her blood-soaked friend. The friend whose very first thought had been to sacrifice herself as a protective shield.

Unlike in movies where the mourner screamed for someone to call an ambulance, Shawna thought to grab her phone and make the call herself.

"9-1-1, what is your emergency?"

"My friend got shot and she need help bad!"

"Is your friend still breathing, ma'am?"

"I don't know. But I don't think so. She got blood everywhere, and she won't answer me. Please help me."

"Ma'am, if I could just—"

With her falling tears blending with the blood on Asha's face, Shawna dropped the phone, cradled Asha's head in her arms and cried, "Please, don't leave me, girl. I ain't ready yet. What we gon' do without you? Come on, Asha, please wake up."

As the blare of sirens could be heard in the distance, Shawna held on to Asha and gently rocked her; just as Asha had done with her on the day they first met.

Chapter 21

Harper University Hospital

You couldn't quite understand what she said, but Noni could be heard before she was seen. When she marched into the ER's waiting room with Double-O on her heels, a sobbing Shawna hopped up and hurried to meet her. "Noni, it should've been me. It should've been me, Noni."

Noni moved Shawna aside and went up to the front desk. "I need to see my sister, Asha Kincaid."

"Ma'am, I'm afraid that can't happen right now. But if you'll be patient, a doctor will be out to speak with you, shortly."

Noni leaned closer to the woman and lowered her voice. "Do you got a family at home?" The woman nodded, to which Noni forewarned, "Well, if you wanna see them again, then I suggest you make sure I get to see mine. Now where the fuck her room at?"

Before the nurse could decline or comply, a doctor entered the waiting area with a chart in his hand. "Is there a Noni Kincaid present?"

"That's me." She ran over to him.

The doctor explained that Asha had been shot a total of five times, with the most critical being the one to her head. The bullet went through-and-through, but had grazed the cerebrum in the process, which had caused a massive swelling of the brain.

"Doc, I don't understand all that medical shit. Just tell me she gon' be alright."

"If I did, I'd be lying. Ma'am, you have to understand that your sister suffered a horrific injury, that not very many have been fortunate to survive. She's presently in a coma, with a respirator serving as her primary source of oxygen. So, no, Ms. Kincaid, I can't offer any guarantees that your sister will be fine, or even make it through the night. But I can say, if you're a religious person, now's the time you may wanna pray."

The doctor turned and walked off and Noni caught up to him. "I need to ser her, doc."

"She's in a coma, Ms. Kincaid. She can't see you or hear you, so it would be of no use."

"It's not for her, it's for me. That's my twin, doc. She the only family I got. And I'm begging you, man, please let me see her. Please."

He reluctantly agreed, telling Noni she could view her through the window of her room.

Accompanied by Double-O and Shawna, Noni followed the doctor to Asha's room. In spite of a pounding heart, she kept telling herself she had to stay strong for the sake of her sister.

Upon reaching her room, the doctor stepped back and extended his hand for Noni to look. Inhaling a deep breath for composure and courage, Noni stepped up to the window and peered through its glass.

Noni went breathless at the sight she saw lying in that hospital bed. Bearing a lifeless appearance, Asha's head was wrapped up in a mummy-like manner, and she was hooked up to an assortment of tubes. *That can't be her*, she thought in disbelief of the heartbreaking image. *Oh. My. God.* She eventually turned from the window and stared at Shawna through teary eyes. "How could you let this happen?"

"Noni, I'm sorry. But she grabbed me and—"

"Come look at her," Noni cut her off, as the tears now flowed. "Come look." When Shawna's feet failed to move, Noni loudly repeated, "I said come look at her, Shawna!"

As Shawna covered her mouth to smother a sob, the doctor intervened, "Ma'am, I'ma need you to calm down."

"Calm down?" Noni spun on the doctor. "Calm down? That's my muthafucking twin laid up in there like that, and you talking about calm down? Muthafucka, don't tell me to calm down. Tell me what the fuck you gon' do to fix her!"

"Alright, that's enough. I'ma have to ask you to leave now." As her anguish converted to red-hot rage, Noni lost it, and began throwing and destroying everything within reach.

The doctor grew fearful of her psychotic behavior and fled for his life. This was now a matter for security, and he was simply a surgeon.

Noni was still on a rampage, when a pair of male guards came charging down the hallway, armed with cannisters of mace. "Hey!"

But before they could spray, Double-O smoothly stepped in their path. "You spray her with that shit, and I *promise* I'ma spray you with something that's gon' hurt a whole lot worse."

While neither guard considered himself a coward, Double-O bore the fearsome, emotionless glare like that of a wild animal. And there was no doubt in either man's mind that he'd live up to his promise.

"Well, you need to make her stop if you don't want us to spray," one of the men said in negotiation. "Because she can't be in here tearing up this hospital, man."

With a crowd of spectators observing from afar, Noni was slamming a wheelchair into the wall, when Double-O grabbed her up from behind.

"Let me go!" She violently fought to get loose. "Let me go, nigga!"

As Double-O carried a flailing Noni down the hall, Shawna slid slowly down the wall, buried her head in her lap and convulsively cried. With there being nothing she could do to reverse this calamity, she was thinking to herself, *When it rains, it pours.*

Outside in the parking lot, Double-O calmly sat behind the wheel, as Noni was beside him, staring off into space. There was a fresh crack across the front windshield; as it had taken some time for Noni to calm down. There were no words that would lessen the pain, so Double-O just waited for Noni's directions. And whether she wanted to camp-out at Harper or go on a killing spree, he was all in.

Noni unconsciously toyed with the half-heart pendant her and Asha always wore. Also around her neck was a thin, gold necklace that featured a praying hands pendant. It was the gift Reverend Daniels had given them for their birthday. It was supposedly a source of protection, but Noni couldn't tell. "What I'm supposed to do without my twin, 'O?" She finally spoke, in a daze-like state.

Double-O kept quiet, as he knew this was an instance when no answer was required.

"That girl raised me, and we the same age. She was the mother I never had. She was the big sister I admired. She was the only friend I ever needed. And somebody done took her from me, 'O. They done took out my soul, bro."

As a set of tears slid down her face, Noni reached beneath her seat and came up clutching a full-size Glock which Double-O immediately recognized as Martha.

Noni forced the slide back and fed a round into the gun's chamber. "Is you with me, 'O?"

He looked over at her and emphatically replied, "Forever."

Noni turned to face him, her bloodshot eyes a reflection of fury. "On my twin sister's soul... I'm finna paint this bitch red!"

To be continued…

Lock Down Publications and Ca$h Presents
Assisted Publishing Packages

BASIC PACKAGE	UPGRADED PACKAGE
$499	$800
Editing	Typing
Cover Design	Editing
Formatting	Cover Design
	Formatting
ADVANCE PACKAGE	**LDP SUPREME PACKAGE**
$1,200	$1,500
Typing	Typing
Editing	Editing
Cover Design	Cover Design
Formatting	Formatting
Copyright registration	Copyright registration
Proofreading	Proofreading
Upload book to Amazon	Set up Amazon account
	Upload book to Amazon
	Advertise on LDP, Amazon and Facebook Page

***Other services available upon request.
Additional charges may apply

Lock Down Publications
P.O. Box 944
Stockbridge, GA 30281-9998
Phone: 470 303-9761

Submission Guideline

Submit the first three chapters of your completed manuscript to ldpsubmissions@gmail.com. In the subject line add **Your Book's Title**. The manuscript must be in a Word Doc file and sent as an attachment. Document should be in Times New Roman, double spaced, and in size 12 font. Also, provide your synopsis and full contact information. If sending multiple submissions, they must each be in a separate email.

Have a story but no way to send it electronically? You can still submit to LDP/Ca$h Presents. Send in the first three chapters, written or typed, of your completed manuscript to:

LDP: Submissions Dept
P.O. Box 944
Stockbridge, GA 30281-9998

DO NOT send original manuscript. Must be a duplicate. Provide your synopsis and a cover letter containing your full contact information.

Thanks for considering LDP and Ca$h Presents.

NEW RELEASES

BLOODLINE OF A SAVAGE 1&2
THESE VICIOUS STREETS
RELENTLESS GOON
RELENTLESS GOON 2
BY PRINCE A. TAUHID

THE BUTTERFLY MAFIA 1-3
BY FUMIYA PAYNE

A THUG'S STREET PRINCESS 1&2
BY MEESHA

CITY OF SMOKE 2
BY MOLOTTI

STEPPERS 1,2&3
BY KING RIO

THE LANE 1&2
BY KEN-KEN SPENCE

THUG OF SPADES 1&2
LOVE IN THE TRENCHES 2
BY COREY ROBINSON

TIL DEATH 3
BY ARYANNA

THE BIRTH OF A GANGSTER 4
BY DELMONT PLAYER

PRODUCT OF THE STREETS 1&2
BY DEMOND "MONEY" ANDERSON

NO TIME FOR ERROR
BY KEESE

MONEY HUNGRY DEMONS
BY TRANAY ADAMS

Coming Soon from Lock Down Publications/Ca$h Presents

IF YOU CROSS ME ONCE 6
ANGEL V
By Anthony Fields

IMMA DIE BOUT MINE 4&5
By Aryanna

A THUGS STREET PRINCESS 3
By Meesha

PRODUCT OF THE STREETS 3
By Demond Money Anderson

CORNER BOYS
By Corey Robinson

SON OF A DOPE FIEND 4
By Renta

THE MURDER QUEENS 6&7
By Michael Gallon

CITY OF SMOKE 3
By Molotti

BETRAYAL OF A G
By Ray Vinci

CONFESSIONS OF A DOPE BOY
By Nicholas Lock

THA TAKEOVER
By Keith Chandler

Available Now

RESTRAINING ORDER 1 & 2
By **CA$H & Coffee**

LOVE KNOWS NO BOUNDARIES 1-3
By **Coffee**

RAISED AS A GOON I, II, III & IV
BRED BY THE SLUMS I, II, III
BLAST FOR ME I & II
ROTTEN TO THE CORE I II III
A BRONX TALE I, II, III
DUFFLE BAG CARTEL I II III IV V VI
HEARTLESS GOON I II III IV V
A SAVAGE DOPEBOY I II
DRUG LORDS I II III
CUTTHROAT MAFIA I II
KING OF THE TRENCHES
By **Ghost**

LAY IT DOWN I & II
LAST OF A DYING BREED I II
BLOOD STAINS OF A SHOTTA I & II III
By **Jamaica**

LOYAL TO THE GAME I II III
LIFE OF SIN I, II III
By **TJ & Jelissa**

IF LOVING HIM IS WRONG…I & II
LOVE ME EVEN WHEN IT HURTS I II III
By **Jelissa**

BLOODY COMMAS I & II
SKI MASK CARTEL I, II & III
KING OF NEW YORK I II, III IV V
RISE TO POWER I II III
COKE KINGS I II III IV V
BORN HEARTLESS I II III IV
KING OF THE TRAP I II
By **T.J. Edwards**

WHEN THE STREETS CLAP BACK I & II III
THE HEART OF A SAVAGE I II III IV
MONEY MAFIA I II
LOYAL TO THE SOIL I II III
By **Jibril Williams**

A DISTINGUISHED THUG STOLE MY HEART I II &
III
LOVE SHOULDN'T HURT I II III IV
RENEGADE BOYS 1-4
PAID IN KARMA 1-3
SAVAGE STORMS 1-3
AN UNFORESEEN LOVE 1-3
BABY, I'M WINTERTIME COLD 1-3
A THUG'S STREET PRINCESS 1&2
By **Meesha**

A GANGSTER'S CODE 1-3
A GANGSTER'S SYN 1-3
THE SAVAGE LIFE 1-3
CHAINED TO THE STREETS 1-3
BLOOD ON THE MONEY 1-3
A GANGSTA'S PAIN 1-3
BEAUTIFUL LIES AND UGLY TRUTHS
CHURCH IN THESE STREETS
By **J-Blunt**

PUSH IT TO THE LIMIT
By **Bre' Hayes**

BLOOD OF A BOSS 1-5
SHADOWS OF THE GAME
TRAP BASTARD
By **Askari**

THE STREETS BLEED MURDER 1-3
THE HEART OF A GANGSTA 1-3
By **Jerry Jackson**

CUM FOR ME 1-8
An LDP Erotica Collaboration

BRIDE OF A HUSTLA 1-3
THE FETTI GIRLS 1-3
CORRUPTED BY A GANGSTA 1-4
BLINDED BY HIS LOVE
THE PRICE YOU PAY FOR LOVE 1-3
DOPE GIRL MAGIC 1-3
By **Destiny Skai**

WHEN A GOOD GIRL GOES BAD
By **Adrienne**

A KINGPIN'S AMBITION
A KINGPIN'S AMBITION II
I MURDER FOR THE DOUGH
By **Ambitious**

THE COST OF LOYALTY 1-3
By **Kweli**

A GANGSTER'S REVENGE 1-4
THE BOSS MAN'S DAUGHTERS 1-5
A SAVAGE LOVE 1&2
BAE BELONGS TO ME 1&2
A HUSTLER'S DECEIT 1-3
WHAT BAD BITCHES DO 1-3
SOUL OF A MONSTER 1-3
KILL ZONE
A DOPE BOY'S QUEEN 1-3
TIL DEATH 1-3
IMMA DIE BOUT MINE 1-3
By **Aryanna**

TRUE SAVAGE 1-7
DOPE BOY MAGIC 1-3
MIDNIGHT CARTEL 1-3
CITY OF KINGZ 1&2
NIGHTMARE ON SILENT AVE
THE PLUG OF LIL MEXICO 1&2
CLASSIC CITY
By **Chris Green**

A DOPEBOY'S PRAYER
By **Eddie "Wolf" Lee**

THE KING CARTEL 1-3
By **Frank Gresham**

THESE NIGGAS AIN'T LOYAL 1-3
By **Nikki Tee**

GANGSTA SHYT 1-3
By **CATO**

THE ULTIMATE BETRAYAL
By **Phoenix**

BOSS'N UP 1-3
By **Royal Nicole**

I LOVE YOU TO DEATH
By **Destiny J**

I RIDE FOR MY HITTA
I STILL RIDE FOR MY HITTA
By **Misty Holt**

LOVE & CHASIN' PAPER
By **Qay Crockett**

TO DIE IN VAIN
SINS OF A HUSTLA
By **ASAD**

BROOKLYN HUSTLAZ
By **Boogsy Morina**

BROOKLYN ON LOCK 1 & 2
By **Sonovia**

A DRUG KING AND HIS DIAMOND 1-3
A DOPEMAN'S RICHES
HER MAN, MINE'S TOO 1&2
CASH MONEY HO'S
THE WIFEY I USED TO BE 1&2
PRETTY GIRLS DO NASTY THINGS
By **Nicole Goosby**

LIPSTICK KILLAH 1-3
CRIME OF PASSION 1-3
FRIEND OR FOE 1-3
By **Mimi**

TRAPHOUSE KING 1-3
KINGPIN KILLAZ 1-3
STREET KINGS 1&2
PAID IN BLOOD 1&2
CARTEL KILLAZ 1-3
DOPE GODS 1&2
By **Hood Rich**

STEADY MOBBN' 1-3
THE STREETS STAINED MY SOUL 1-3
By **Marcellus Allen**

WHO SHOT YA 1-3
SON OF A DOPE FIEND 1-3
HEAVEN GOT A GHETTO 1&2
SKI MASK MONEY 1&2
By **Renta**

GORILLAZ IN THE BAY 1-4
TEARS OF A GANGSTA 1/&2
3X KRAZY 1&2
STRAIGHT BEAST MODE 1&2
By **DE'KARI**

TRIGGADALE 1-3
MURDA WAS THE CASE 1-3
By **Elijah R. Freeman**

THE STREETS ARE CALLING
By **Duquie Wilson**

SLAUGHTER GANG 1-3
RUTHLESS HEART 1-3
By **Willie Slaughter**

GANGSTA CITY
By **Teddy Duke**

GOD BLESS THE TRAPPERS 1-3
THESE SCANDALOUS STREETS 1-3
FEAR MY GANGSTA 1-5
THESE STREETS DON'T LOVE NOBODY 1-2
BURY ME A G 1-5
A GANGSTA'S EMPIRE 1-4
THE DOPEMAN'S BODYGAURD 1&2
THE REALEST KILLAZ 1-3
THE LAST OF THE OGS 1-3
By **Tranay Adams**

MARRIED TO A BOSS 1-3
By **Destiny Skai & Chris Green**

KINGZ OF THE GAME 1-7
CRIME BOSS 1-3
By **Playa Ray**

ADDICTED TO THE DRAMA 1-3
IN THE ARM OF HIS BOSS
By **Jamila**

LOYALTY AIN'T PROMISED 1&2
By **Keith Williams**

YAYO 1-4
A SHOOTER'S AMBITION 1&2
BRED IN THE GAME
By **S. Allen**

FUK SHYT
By **Blakk Diamond**

DON'T F#CK WITH MY HEART 1&2
By **Linnea**

TRAP GOD 1-3
RICH $AVAGE 1-3
MONEY IN THE GRAVE 1-3
CARTEL MONEY
By **Martell Troublesome Bolden**

FOREVER GANGSTA 1&2
GLOCKS ON SATIN SHEETS 1&2
By **Adrian Dulan**

TOE TAGZ 1-4
LEVELS TO THIS SHYT 1&2
IT'S JUST ME AND YOU
By **Ah'Million**

KINGPIN DREAMS 1-3
RAN OFF ON DA PLUG
By **Paper Boi Rari**

CONFESSIONS OF A GANGSTA 1-4
CONFESSIONS OF A JACKBOY 1-3
CONFESSIONS OF A HITMAN
By **Nicholas Lock**

I'M NOTHING WITHOUT HIS LOVE
SINS OF A THUG
TO THE THUG I LOVED BEFORE
A GANGSTA SAVED XMAS
IN A HUSTLER I TRUST
By **Monet Dragun**

QUIET MONEY 1-3
THUG LIFE 1-3
EXTENDED CLIP 1&2
A GANGSTA'S PARADISE
By **Trai'Quan**

CAUGHT UP IN THE LIFE 1-3
THE STREETS NEVER LET GO 1-3
By **Robert Baptiste**

NEW TO THE GAME 1-3
MONEY, MURDER & MEMORIES 1-3
By **Malik D. Rice**

CREAM 2-3
THE STREETS WILL TALK
By **Yolanda Moore**

LIFE OF A SAVAGE 1-4
A GANGSTA'S QUR'AN 1-4
MURDA SEASON 1-3
GANGLAND CARTEL 1-3
CHI'RAQ GANGSTAS 1-4
KILLERS ON ELM STREET 1-3
JACK BOYZ N DA BRONX 1-3
A DOPEBOY'S DREAM 1-3
JACK BOYS VS DOPE BOYS 1-3
COKE GIRLZ
COKE BOYS
SOSA GANG 1&2
BRONX SAVAGES
BODYMORE KINGPINS
BLOOD OF A GOON
By **Romell Tukes**

THE STREETS MADE ME 1-3
By **Larry D. Wright**

CONCRETE KILLA 1-3
VICIOUS LOYALTY 1-3
By **Kingpen**

THE ULTIMATE SACRIFICE 1-6
KHADIFI
IF YOU CROSS ME ONCE 1-3
ANGEL 1-4
IN THE BLINK OF AN EYE
By **Anthony Fields**

THE LIFE OF A HOOD STAR
By **Ca$h & Rashia Wilson**

THE STREETS WILL NEVER CLOSE 1-3
By **K'ajji**

NIGHTMARES OF A HUSTLA 1-3
By **King Dream**

HARD AND RUTHLESS 1&2
MOB TOWN 251
THE BILLIONAIRE BENTLEYS 1-3
REAL G'S MOVE IN SILENCE
By **Von Diesel**

GHOST MOB
By **Stilloan Robinson**

MOB TIES 1-6
SOUL OF A HUSTLER, HEART OF A KILLER 1-3
GORILLAZ IN THE TRENCHES
By **SayNoMore**

BODYMORE MURDERLAND 1-3
THE BIRTH OF A GANGSTER 1-4
By **Delmont Player**

FOR THE LOVE OF A BOSS 1&2
By **C. D. Blue**

KILLA KOUNTY 1-5
By **Khufu**

MOBBED UP 1-4
THE BRICK MAN 1-5
THE COCAINE PRINCESS 1-10
STEPPERS 1-3
SUPER GREMLIN 1-4
By **King Rio**

MONEY GAME 1&2
By **Smoove Dolla**

A GANGSTA'S KARMA 1-4
By **FLAME**

KING OF THE TRENCHES 1-3
By **GHOST & TRANAY ADAMS**

QUEEN OF THE ZOO 1&2
By **Black Migo**

GRIMEY WAYS 1-3
By **Ray Vinci**

XMAS WITH AN ATL SHOOTER
By **Ca$h & Destiny Skai**

THE BUTTERFLY MAFIA 3 | FUMIYA PAYNE

KING KILLA 1&2
By **Vincent "Vitto" Holloway**

BETRAYAL OF A THUG 1&2
By **Fre$h**

THE MURDER QUEENS 1-5
By **Michael Gallon**

FOR THE LOVE OF BLOOD 1-4
By **Jamel Mitchell**

HOOD CONSIGLIERE 1&2
NO TIME FOR ERROR
By **Keese**

PROTÉGÉ OF A LEGEND 1&2
LOVE IN THE TRENCHES 1&2
By **Corey Robinson**

BORN IN THE GRAVE 1-3
CRIME PAYS
By **Self Made Tay**

MOAN IN MY MOUTH
By **XTASY**

TORN BETWEEN A GANGSTER AND A GENTLEMAN
By **J-BLUNT & Miss Kim**

LOYALTY IS EVERYTHING 1-3
CITY OF SMOKE 1&2
By **Molotti**

HERE TODAY GONE TOMORROW 1&2
By **Fly Rock**

WOMEN LIE MEN LIE 1-4
FIFTY SHADES OF SNOW 1-3
STACK BEFORE YOU SPLURGE
GIRLS FALL LIKE DOMINOES
NAÏVE TO THE STREETS
By **ROY MILLIGAN**

PILLOW PRINCESS
By **S. Hawkins**

THE BUTTERFLY MAFIA 1-3
SALUTE MY SAVAGERY 1&2
By **Fumiya Payne**

THE LANE 1&2
By Ken-Ken Spence

THE PUSSY TRAP 1-5
By **Nene Capri**

DIRTY DNA
By **Blaque**

SANCTIFIED AND HORNY
by **XTASY**